CW00501527

THE VISCOUNT'S UNLIKELY ALLY (ONLY FOR LOVE BOOK 4)

A CLEAN REGENCY ROMANCE

ROSE PEARSON

THE VISCOUNT'S UNLIKELY ALLY

PROLOGUE

*P*hillip grinned in delight as he walked into White's, hearing the cheer that went up from a few of the other gentlemen. How he had missed this! The rest of the year had been taken up with annoying responsibilities which he could not avoid, with the winter being very dreary and grey indeed. Now, however, he was back within society, back to where he might indulge himself and be as much of a scoundrel as he wished to be. After all, what else was there for him to consider?

"I see you have returned a little earlier than you said you expected to." Lord Marchmont lifted an eyebrow "Your eagerness was such that you could not hold back, I suppose."

Phillip chuckled good-naturedly and swung himself down into the seat beside Lord Marchmont. They had long been friends and, although Lord Marchmont did not approve of all that Phillip did, they were still very closely acquainted.

"I completed my remaining duties as quickly as I could, if that is what you are asking, yes."

"Simply so you could make your way to London a few days earlier than you had anticipated?"

Again, Phillip laughed and shrugged.

"It seems so! How glad my heart is to be back amongst everyone! I have found this last year very trying in many ways, I confess."

Lacking any sort of sympathy, his friend rolled his eyes.

"That is only because you have been forced to take on the responsibilities which your father once managed, and you do not much like it! This has been your third year of holding the title, has it not?" His eyebrow lifted again. "One might imagine that you would have become used to your responsibilities by now. It is not as easy to be a rogue when one is a Viscount."

Sighing heavily at this, Phillip lifted his hand to catch the attention of the footman, telling him to bring a brandy for them both.

"Alas, Marchmont, you may be disappointed in me," he told his friend. "I, for one, have every intention of simply enjoying being present here in London, alongside my many good friends and acquaintances."

"And amongst the very many beautiful ladies who will capture your attention, no doubt."

This slightly scornful remark was followed by one from another gentleman, who waved one hand to catch his attention.

"I should say so! That is the hope of every gentleman, is it not? To have ourselves *caught* by a beautiful lady... for however long we permit ourselves to be so!"

Phillip immediately looked at the man, then laughed aloud.

"Indeed, Lord Wesley." Phillip accepted his brandy, a

broad smile settling onto his face. "My dear friend Lord Marchmont insists on calling me a rogue, and perhaps that is what I am. I do not feel any particular shame over it, for to my eyes, I am simply a gentleman who enjoys company. *Fine* company, in fact, and if that should bring with it a little warmth, then what cause have I to complain?" This statement was met by some exclamations and cheers of agreement as many of the other fellows in White's gave him their attention, as his voice had rung around the room. Lord Marchmont, however, simply shook his head, his smile fading to a grimace. Phillip attempted to pay him very little heed. "Not all of us are sober-minded," he continued, chuckling as many of the other gentlemen nodded firmly, murmuring their agreement, tapping their empty glasses upon the table as though to concur. "Not all of us are here to wed. Some of us come to society for a little enjoyment, a little pleasure - and I do not think that our requirements should be looked upon with any sort of disdain. After all, we have worked hard these last few months, fulfilling our responsibilities, and setting a firm hand to our estate. Why should we not indulge ourselves a little? Why should we not enjoy all that London society has to offer us?"

Again, the room rang with the sound of agreement, although some, Phillip noticed, averted their eyes and smiled indulgently. Those who did so, he considered, were the gentlemen who were very much inclined to wed this Season. A slight pang of sympathy chimed in his heart for them.

Those poor fools. How much they will lose in tying themselves to one particular young lady.

"I see you intend to use this Season in much the same way as you did the last." Lord Marchmont sighed as Phillip shrugged both shoulders, still grinning. "Recall, you did make quite a name for yourself last Season and, might I be bold enough to suggest, not all of it was good."

"I should be vastly disappointed if it was all good." Phillip picked up his brandy glass. "This may come as a surprise to you, but your notes of concern will do very little to change me or my expectations for these next few months."

Lord Marchmont shook his head.

"I did not think that anything I said would have any sort of impact," he responded quickly. "There is one thing I *shall* say, however, which comes from the Bible." Phillip sobered quickly, for he was not about to laugh at something so sacred, but at the same time, silently steeled himself for what was to come. "I believe it says, 'Be sure your sins will find you out'." Lord Marchmont paused, letting his words weigh heavily on Phillip. "I believe that to be very true for, in this case, if you continue as you intend – indulging yourself and the like, then what will become of you? Be cautious, my friend. You may have enjoyed yourself last Season, but I am certain that you cannot be entirely unaware of those you injured."

A thread of guilt threatened to push itself like a needle into Phillip's heart, but he quickly brushed it aside.

"Save your piety for someone else," he shot back rather brusquely. "I have no time for it."

Lord Marchmont did not seem at all insulted, merely shrugging and accepting that this was Phillip's response to the warning he had given him. Phillip turned his head away, making to speak with Lord Wesley instead. He became irritated, however, to realize that Lord Marchmont's words were lingering in his mind. Even though he threw himself into jovial conversation, they still fastened themselves there. Was his friend correct? Would this be the Season where his own hedonistic choices brought heavy consequences for him?

CHAPTER ONE

"And now, we come to the Season where you must find a husband."

Deborah offered her mother a brief smile.

"Yes, Mama, I am aware of father's expectations."

She glanced at her reflection only briefly, turning her gaze away and smiling again at her mother. Lady Prescott had spent a great deal of time making certain that Deborah was ready for the London Season, just as she had done the previous year, *and* as she had done with Deborah's elder sisters. To look upon herself, ready for her second Season in London – the Season where she was to find a husband – Deborah had to admit that she did not immediately recognize herself, for her mother's efforts were quite transforming. Some special hair soap had been procured and Deborah's fair hair seemed now to shine with a soft golden glow, so when the sun glinted upon it, it became almost vivid with her curls hanging beautifully. While there had been a great deal of fuss over her complexion during the previous months, and Deborah had become a little irritated by all of her mother's machinations, it appeared to have done very well for her. A gentle pink seemed to rest always in her cheeks and her blue eyes were framed by soft, delicate lashes. She had to hope that the gentlemen of London would consider her becoming, at the very least!

"This is the Season for consideration and caution," Lady Prescott reminded her. "Last Season was a time for enjoyment, a time for making new acquaintances, for dancing and for laughter, but now, however, you must think of your future."

Deborah nodded.

"I understand, Mama. Thank you for all that you have done to prepare me, both last Season and this."

Lady Prescott smiled softly.

"I swore that I should care for all of my daughters in the same way, that I would treat each with the same level of dedication as the others. I am glad that your elder sisters have found success, and I am certain, my dear Deborah, that you will also find yourself a suitable gentleman very soon. And you must thank your father also," she finished, a gentle gleam in her eye. "For he is the one who has paid for all of your new gowns and fripperies – though I think he dared not even question how much I have spent! He knows better than to do so!" Deborah laughed, reached out, and squeezed her mother's hand as she stood a little to the right of Deborah, looking out of the window. She adored both of her parents. Her father was a strong gentleman in matters of business, but certainly a quiet fellow to his wife and his daughters. Her mother was very similar – a gentle spirit but firm with it. There had been times in her childhood where Deborah had overheard her mother and father discussing something at great length, and with sharp tones which, she had learned, was rather unexpected of a lady of quality. Now, however, she was grateful for it. Her mother had taught her what it was like to be a refined lady but also to have one's own strength of character. "I suppose you will be continuing your acquaintance with Lady Yardley and your friends?" Lady Prescott smiled and tilted her head. "I have a great deal of respect for Lady Yardley, I confess."

Deborah nodded.

"As do I. If you and Father are contented with it, I should like to continue my acquaintance with her."

Her mother's smile grew.

"But of course. I should be glad to become a little better acquainted with her myself. She still writes 'The London Ledger', does she not?"

"Yes, she does. I do appreciate how truthful she is with it. Anything she writes that may be rumor is stated to be so and is only put there as a warning, either to the gentleman or lady in question – or to those who may be acquainted with that person. Otherwise, it is simply delightful bits of news and messages from abroad. It does not contain a hint of scandal, for which I am very grateful."

Her mother sat down opposite her for a moment as Deborah continued to sit on the stool at her dressing table.

"I do want you to be careful, my dear." She smiled softly. "I noted in the Ledger only last week that Lady Yardley had mentioned the return of Lord Brookmire."

A slight frown crossed Deborah's forehead.

"I do not think I know the name. What was said about him?"

Lady Prescott laughed softly.

"That is just it. Nothing was said about him other than to note he was returned to London. I believe Lady Yardley hoped that his reputation would speak for itself."

Deborah's frown grew.

"Either he is an excellent gentleman with a sterling

reputation, in which case all young unmarried ladies of quality ought to take note of his arrival, or he is a scoundrel with a despicable reputation, and all young ladies of the *ton* ought to take steps to avoid him." She lifted one eyebrow. "Which is it?"

Her mother laughed softly.

"That was very well put, my dear, but I am afraid it is the latter." Her smile faded. "You must make every effort to avoid Lord Brookmire when he appears. He may attempt to introduce himself to you and of course, if such a situation should occur, then we will be polite, but short in our conversation. You are not to indulge him."

Deborah nodded.

"I understand, Mama, and will be most careful around Lord Brookmire. I am quite certain that he will have very little interest in introducing himself to me, however."

Her mother arched an eyebrow.

"I think you might be mistaken there, Deborah." A light smile touched the corners of her mouth, though it faded quickly. "You are young and beautiful, and unfortunately, Lord Brookmire has no hesitation in seeking the attentions of young unmarried ladies." With a shake of her head, she rose to her feet. "I do not want to ever see you dancing with him or the like."

"And I can assure you, I will never step into his arms," Deborah declared. "I am quite certain, Mama, that you have nothing to worry about when it comes to Lord Brookmire. It will be easy enough to stay far away from him."

"There are many fine gentlemen at the ball, are there not?"

Deborah smiled, her eyes roving around the room as she considered her friend's remark. Thus far, she had to admit that, yes, the ball did seem to be very pleasing indeed. Lady Almeria was now dancing with an old friend, someone she had not seen in some years, while Deborah and Lady Elizabeth stood together. They did not have anyone to dance with for this particular dance, but the rest of Deborah's card was almost full, which left her with contented satisfaction.

"Did you see what Lady Yardley wrote in the most recent Ledger?" Lady Elizabeth asked with a wry smile. "I assume one gentleman in particular will not be pleased!"

Turning interested eyes to her friend, Deborah tipped her head.

"You speak of Lord Brookmire, I assume?" Seeing her nod, she shrugged. "I confess that I do not know the gentleman at all. My mother has recently informed me of him and his reputation."

Lady Elizabeth laughed softly.

"You are blessed indeed to be entirely unaware of him. Quite how you avoided his gaze last Season I cannot explain, for you are quite beautiful and just the sort of young lady he would seek."

Shaking her head, Deborah threw Lady Elizabeth a glance.

"You are very kind."

"And yet, quite serious," Lady Elizabeth continued firmly. "You need not hide back in the shadow of your sisters any longer. Your mother has clearly made a great deal of effort when it comes to your appearance, both last Season and this. You should be quite pleased. I am sure that a gentleman will seek you for his bride very soon."

Giggling, Deborah put one hand to her mouth to hide her smile.

"So long as it is not Lord Brookmire, then I shall be contented." She tilted her head, her smile fading. "And so long as I find myself in love with the gentleman in question, and he with me."

Lady Elizabeth nodded.

"Of course."

Only last Season, Deborah, Lady Elizabeth, and their other dear friends had made a promise, that when it came time for them to wed, they would seek only a gentleman who loved them rather than marrying for the sake of convenience – and Lady Yardley was now also supporting them in whatever way she could.

"I can assure you that certainly will *not* be Lord Brookmire." Lady Elizabeth's smile was wry. "That gentleman cares nothing for affection, or even for the feelings of others!" Her lips pursed for a moment. "Last Season was the first which he attended, after his mourning following his father's death. His first since he became Viscount Brookmire. However, he made it quite clear that he was to throw aside all of his responsibilities and thereafter take as much pleasure as he wished during the Season. He did whatever he wanted, and in whatever way he wished, and thus, the feelings and considerations of others were not even a thought to him. That is why Lady Yardley mentioned his return in the Ledger, although I noted that she said nothing about his previous behavior, nor the names attached to him."

Deborah sighed.

"Which is precisely what we would expect from Lady Yardley, is it not? I am grateful to her for it." She smiled softly. "Lady Yardley is a lady of integrity. She will not write anything about a person's character within the Ledger unless it is entirely necessary and, if it is a whisper, then she will always state as much. I do admire her for that."

"In this case, the warning is clear, even without her saying anything specific," Lady Elizabeth added. "Those of us who are aware of his reputation already know to stay away from him, and those who do not know, such as yourself, are then informed by friends, so that you might do the very same."

Glancing across to where her mother stood only a short distance away, Deborah found herself smiling briefly. The concern of both her parents and her friends was touching.

"As I have already said to my mother, I have no intention of going anywhere near Lord Brookmire."

"Well, that would be a pity, since I am very pleasant indeed!"

A deep voice interrupted her conversation, but it was with a sharp glance that Deborah looked at the gentleman who had stopped before them. She took him in quickly, seeing his well-built figure, his slightly tilted chin, gleaming green eyes, and thick brown hair which flashed with hints of red where the candlelight touched it. His features were quite pleasing, of course, but it was not that which dissuaded her from him. Instead, it was the broad smile that settled on his features, the arrogance within that look that had her stomach turning over. She did not doubt that she stood in the presence of the very gentleman of whom they had been speaking.

And I am not about to melt with either embarrassment or appreciation for his handsomeness.

"I do not think that we have been introduced."

With a tilt of her chin, Deborah narrowed her eyes a little, then turned her head away directly. It was a distinct and all-encompassing gesture, making it quite clear to the gentleman that she had no desire to speak with him further.

His response, however, was to chuckle.

"Indeed, we have not." The gentleman's grin, and following laughter when she shot him a glance, had her face flushing hot - but not with great delight at his attention. Instead, it was with anger that his arrogance should be displayed so toward her. "I can easily remedy that, for you and I have been acquainted, Lady Elizabeth. Would you not introduce me to your fair companion, who seemingly wishes to have no interest in my company, even though she and I have never so much as a single word to each other?"

Deborah opened her mouth to state that she had no interest in acquainting herself with a gentleman whose poor reputation preceded him, only to snap it shut again, fearing that he was attempting to goad her into responding before it was appropriate for her to do so.

Lady Elizabeth let out a small harrumph.

"I shall do so simply because I am bound by the rules of propriety, not because I have any wish to do so," came her sharp response. "Lord Brookmire, might I present Miss Deborah Madeley, daughter to Viscount Prescott. Miss Madeley, this is the Viscount Brookmire."

"*Delighted* to make your acquaintance."

Lord Brookmire grinned, sweeping into a great bow. It was the expected response, of course, but Deborah herself gave no such murmur. Instead, she smiled briefly but did not let it warm her expression, keeping her eyes averted from him for as long as she could. She caught her mother's gaze as she rose from her curtsey, seeing Lady Prescott frown, then lift an eyebrow in question. Deborah managed a minute shake of her head. No, she did not require her mother's aid at present. Just because Lord Brookmire stood here did not mean that she would have a great long conversation with him. Appreciating her mother's confidence in her – for Lady Prescott did not make a direct step towards her, Deborah finally looked towards Lord Brookmire. He was simply gazing at her with that irritating smirk still plastered across his face, and his eyebrows lifted as though he were waiting for her to finally give him her attention.

"You will not speak with me, then?" Lord Brookmire threw up his hands and feigned exasperation. "You will not ask me whether I have enjoyed the ball, how long I have been in London, or what my intentions are for the Season."

Deborah looked back at him steadily, her gaze unbroken by even a blink.

"No, I shall not, for fear I would give the impression of interest."

Lord Brookmire did not recoil, however. Instead, he let out a bark of laughter and threw back his head.

"Goodness, Miss Madeley, you are a sharp-tongued thing."

Deborah did not flinch.

"Or perhaps it is that you are simply unused to young ladies speaking to you with such honesty, Lord Brookmire," she replied firmly. "You will find that I have no eagerness for conversation with you. I have no interest in your company, and I have every intention of remaining as far from you as I can during the Season."

The smile which had been permanently stuck to Lord Brookmire's face throughout the entirety of the conversation thus far immediately began to weaken.

"You seek to injure me, I think."

Deborah let out a short laugh, her hands going to her hips, her head tilting to the left just a little. She cared not whether she wounded him, but that was not her true desire.

The only thing she wished for at present was to be entirely honest, so that Lord Brookmire would not linger in her company - not for this ball or for any ball thereafter.

"If you take injury from my honest words Lord Brookmire, I cannot help that." Her hands dropped to her sides. "I will not refrain, however."

Lord Brookmire's expression faded still further, a glint of steel coming into his eyes.

"You are quite right, Miss Madeley. I have *never* met a young lady such as yourself, who is so free with her words. Perhaps you might consider yourself a little improper to speak so unreservedly."

Unable to help herself, Deborah let out a short exclamation of laughter, taking no slight from his words.

"I hardly think a gentleman such as yourself, who holds such a *particular* reputation, could even imagine speaking the word 'improper' to anyone!" Her lip curled as darkness ran through his expression. "Were you an upstanding, honest, well regarded, well respected, and honorable fellow, then of course, I would take your words with great consideration... but then again, I would never speak to a gentleman with such qualities in the way I have done with you. I am afraid, Lord Brookmire, that I do not take my words back. I do not offer even the smallest word of apology for them, and my statement as regards placing a great deal of distance between us remains." Flicking her fingers towards him as though shooing him away, she sniffed lightly. "I do not think that we have any further need for conversation. There will be many a young lady eager for your company and I suggest that you may enjoy the ball a good deal more if you linger in company with one of them."

There was a great cloud of tension that swelled between herself and Lord Brookmire as she finished her statement.

Lord Brookmire's face had gone very white, with only a tiny hint of color on either cheek. Deborah did not doubt that he was very angry with what she had said to him, but she did not care. Speaking so would make certain that the gentleman would never again come into her company willingly, which was precisely what she wanted.

Lord Brookmire's lips flattened and he lifted his chin, his jaw jutting forward. He opened his mouth to say something, only to then let out a huff of breath and turn away directly. As he marched across the ballroom, Deborah let out a slow breath that she had not been aware she had been holding.

"Good gracious." Lady Elizabeth put one hand to her heart, then giggled. "I do not think he will return to your side! I must say, you spoke very honestly to him there."

"Which is what is required with a gentleman such as he," Deborah answered, allowing the cloud of tension to dissipate. "I am confident now that Lord Brookmire will never seek out my company again, not after such a conversation."

Lady Elizabeth laughed again and linked one arm through Deborah's.

"Indeed, I am sure that you have pushed him away from you for the rest of your life! But what a very unpleasant gentleman he is."

Deborah nodded, a light smile of victory on her lips.

"I could not agree more."

CHAPTER TWO

"*A*nother."

Scowling, Phillip picked up the brandy glass the moment it was set down on the table before him. Taking a draught, he let his eyes rove around the glass, studying the amber elixir within, wishing it would do what he had intended it to do. This was his third measure since he had arrived at White's after the ball, and as yet, his meeting with Miss Madeley had not faded from his mind.

It has been his first ball of the Season. The first ball where he was to enjoy himself, to make merry, and to lose himself in all manner of delight. Instead, in the first quarter of an hour, he had met one of the most unpleasant, sharp-tongued young ladies he had ever had the opportunity to be introduced to. What was all the more frustrating was that he could not seem to forget the way that she had spoken to him. It was most uncommon and, to his mind, highly improper for a young lady... but then again, he recalled, he could not criticize any impropriety in the behavior of another.

Wincing, he took another sip of his brandy. Miss Madeley had been correct to throw that back into his face, as much as he'd had no wish to accept it at the time. Yes, such things had been said to him before – most recently, Lord Marchmont had spoken to him about the reputation which Phillip was garnering for himself – but he had not reacted as strongly to Lord Marchmont as he now did to Miss Madeley. Why such a thing should be, Phillip did not know, and he tried to tell himself firmly that he did not care, only for her face to return to his mind.

It had not been pride, but almost an insolence which had filled her features. Her eyes had flashed, her lips had continually settled into a moue of dislike and her sharp turns of the head and her unwillingness to hold his gaze spoke of a clear dislike. She would not be the only young lady unwilling to linger in his company, of course, but to have her speak so sharply to him, and with such vehemence, was most displeasing. It was not as though he expected, nor wanted every young lady in the *ton* to be delighted with him and, certainly, he did not anticipate that every lady would willingly throw herself into his arms the moment he opened them, but neither did he want there to be such obvious disparagement.

He rolled his eyes at himself.

Except that is the life of a rogue, is it not?

That consideration gave him no relief from his current thoughts and, try as he might, he could not push the beautiful Miss Madeley away from his awareness. Sighing, Phillip closed his eyes and ran his fingers heavily over his forehead. Yes, he admitted silently, Miss Madeley was indeed beautiful. It was plain for everyone to see, himself included. The heart-shaped face, the fair curls which ran into twists and braids, tendrils brushing her temples, the rosebud lips, the piercing eyes... it was all most appealing. No, he had not been blind to her pleasing features, it was only her manner which had disturbed him.

"You look most despondent."

Lord Anderton, a rather portly gentleman with thinning hair and a smile that Phillip did not like, sat down in a chair next to him, both uninvited and a little unwelcome.

"It is the end of the ball." Phillip answered quickly, having no intention of sharing with Lord Anderton what he was really thinking. "Thus, I am a little glum."

It was a foolish excuse, but one Lord Anderton seemed to accept, given his grin.

"A gentleman after my own heart." He patted his chest as Phillip finished his brandy. "Perhaps I might take away some of your disappointment with a little wager?"

Tilting his head, Phillip looked back at Lord Anderton. He was not well acquainted with him but knew by reputation that Lord Anderton was forever placing bets and wagers, and usually having to pay out a great deal thereafter. He was not a man blessed with either good fortune or wit.

"A wager?"

Lord Anderton nodded, waving to the footman to bring them both another glass.

"Yes, a wager. I am always keeping myself amused with such things, and in this, it appears as though your reputation and my interest in betting might easily align themselves." Not immediately willing to jump into this opportunity, Phillip waited for Lord Anderton to continue before expressing even an ounce of interest. "There is a lady," Lord Anderton began, taking the glass from the footman and throwing back his brandy in only one gulp before continuing. "It is said that she cannot be lured by any gentleman. She has already been wed before but has not sought out the company of any other since her husband's demise some five years ago. She attends balls, soirees, and the like but no, she will not be found in the arms of anyone." Phillip lifted an eyebrow, already anticipating what was to come. "If you can pull her into your arms if you can place a kiss upon her lips, then you shall win the wager. If she refuses you, however, then you will lose."

Considering this, Phillip cleared his throat.

"And how many attempts would I be given?"

Chuckling, Lord Anderton held up one hand, palm out.

"You only have the one opportunity, old boy. Perhaps choosing the right moment would help? A darkened room or catching her when she is taking the air after a dance at the ball? But no, you should only have one opportunity and I must be present to witness it, for I do not believe I should take your word for it."

Grinning, Phillip spread out both hands, his brandy on the table.

"You mean to say that you do not trust me?"

"Certainly I do not, just as you should not trust me." Lord Anderton grinned as Phillip chuckled. "What say you, then? Will you accept my challenge? Will you accept my wager?"

Taking a few steady breaths, Phillip allowed himself a few more moments to think. It would be a good distraction, he considered, and it might help him to forget about Miss Madeley.

"It depends on how much you are willing to wager."

Quickly, Lord Anderton named a sum which made Phillip catch his breath. He did not display this outwardly, however, making sure that Lord Anderton did not see his startled expression by, instead, running a hand over his chin. Slowly, he thought to himself, allowing a few more moments to pass before finally, with a great sigh, he nodded.

"You mean to say, you accept?"

"Yes, I –" Frowning, Phillip sat up a little straighter in his chair. "I *would* accept, so long as I know the name of the lady first and so long as I find her acceptable."

Lord Anderton chuckled darkly, his eyes a little narrowed despite his laughter.

"And I thought to you, all ladies were of equal worth!" He laughed again before Phillip could respond, then shrugged. "Very well. It is Lady Allanthorpe."

Phillip considered the name but quickly realized that he did not know of whom Lord Anderton spoke. She might be well respected among society which, would make his attempt a little more difficult – but, then again, she might be barely known to anyone. His mouth tugged to one side. Surely all he needed to consider at the moment was whether or not he had enough confidence in himself to win the wager.

I am sure I can steal a kiss from this lady, whoever she may be.

His shoulders straightened and he found himself smiling. Lord Anderton was willing to wager a great deal and, if he was foolish enough to bet such a large sum against Phillip on a matter such as this, then it seemed almost wrong not to take advantage of that!

"Very well. I accept your wager. I shall seek out this particular lady and find a suitable opportunity to encourage her into my arms." Grinning, he tilted his head. "However, If you are unwilling to take my word as truth, then you shall have to remain close to me at the next few social occasions,

THE VISCOUNT'S UNLIKELY ALLY | 25

so that I might take advantage of the perfect moment when it offers itself to me."

Lord Anderton laughed, but Phillip's smile fell, for it was not a sound he appreciated. Rather, he inwardly recoiled from it, taking in the glint which had appeared in Lord Anderton's eyes. Yes, he felt confident enough in his endeavor to win the wager but, all the same, Lord Anderton's expression was not pleasing.

"I hardly think that will be of any difficulty," the gentleman told him, once his laughter had died away. "You are usually a very easy fellow to find. All I need to do is look to where the ladies are pulling their daughters away from you as you meander around the ballroom!"

This was said with yet another raucous laugh at the end of it, but Phillip did not even attempt to muster a smile. Those words stung and, despite the fact they were somewhat true, he did not much like hearing them.

"Perhaps I should not ask what causes you so much mirth."

Phillip turned his head at the voice, to find Lord Marchmont, and was filled with relief that his friend was coming to join them for, in doing so, he was saving Phillip from lingering in conversation with Lord Anderton for much longer.

"No, no. Nothing at all." Lord Anderton waved a hand, making it quite clear that he had no intention of speaking of what he and Phillip had discussed. "I will remove myself now, for our conversation is at an end. Good evening, Lord Marchmont, Lord Brookmire."

He rose from the table and left Phillip and Lord Marchmont to speak together, with Phillip letting out a long breath and then turning with a smile to Lord Marchmont. His friend, however, was frowning.

"I do not much like that fellow."

Surprised, Phillip arched an eyebrow.

"It is not like you to be so openly disparaging."

Lord Marchmont chuckled, although his eyes did not light with humor.

"I am not being disparaging. I am being truthful, for I am quite certain that Lord Anderton is not all he appears to be."

"Lord Anderton is *precisely* who he appears to be," Phillip retorted, firmly, "which is why I have accepted his offer of a wager."

The moment he said those words, however, he regretted having done so, for Lord Marchmont's frown darkened all the more, his gaze shot to Phillip and he immediately began to shake his head.

"No, you ought not to have done. That is most unwise."

"And yet I have done so," Phillip interrupted, not wanting another lecture from Lord Marchmont about what he ought or ought not to do. "I have no doubt that you will tell me my reputation is already damaged and I should not do more to mortify myself, but I care nothing for that. I intend to enjoy my time here in London, as I have said, and taking on a few wagers is a part of that."

Again, Lord Marchmont shook his head but this time his lip curled.

"No doubt you will not listen to me regardless," he said slowly. "But I say such things not to make you feel small and insignificant as regards your character, but only because I am concerned. As I have said, Lord Anderton is not a gentleman I trust, and I do not think it wise for you to accept his company either. To take on a wager against him is unwise in the extreme. Have you not heard about Lord Belfast?" He rubbed one hand over his chin. "I am sure you have not, else you would not have taken on such a wager so quickly."

Phillip frowned.

"Lord Belfast?" Something tied itself tightly in his stomach. "I know of him, of course, but he is not in London this Season."

Lord Marchmont rolled his eyes.

"And no doubt, so wrapped up were you in your own sense of contentment and enjoyment last Season, you neither saw nor noticed the plight of others." Phillip opened his mouth to protest, but Lord Marchmont continued firmly. "Lord Belfast took on a wager against Lord Anderton – it was Lord Anderton's suggestion, of course, and was to do with a race between himself and Lord Anderton. Everyone was quite certain that Lord Belfast would win, for his phaeton was of higher quality and his greys much superior to Lord Anderton's. Indeed, Lord Anderton was known to make ridiculous wagers and to lose a good many of them but, in this case, he offered a ridiculously large sum as his bet and every gentleman in London encouraged Lord Belfast to accept." Phillip listened carefully, his heart quickening and all too aware that he had just done the very same thing. Lord Anderton had made a foolishly large bet and Phillip, believing that he was more than likely to be victorious, had quickly and easily accepted. "I do not know precisely what happened." Lord Marchmont's expression was grave, his gaze sticking fast to Phillip's. "I was not myself present, but everyone was talking about it in the days and weeks thereafter."

Taking a breath, Phillip frowned.

"You mean to say that Lord Anderton won this wager? His phaeton and horses were not as low in quality as was believed?"

Lord, Marchmont shook his head.

"That is not to say that Lord Anderton did not win. Yes, he did, but it was only because one of the wheels to Lord Belfast's phaeton began to wobble as the gentleman was racing. It grew worse and worse and, just as Lord Anderton crossed the finish line – well before Lord Belfast, I might add - Lord Belfast was thrown from the phaeton and the wheel came off entirely."

A knot formed in Phillip's stomach, but he tried to chase it away by merely shrugging one shoulder.

"That could very easily have been a defect in the phaeton, and it does not state firmly that Lord Anderton was to blame for it."

Lord Marchmont's closed his eyes as he let out an exasperated sigh.

"What gentleman would not have checked his phaeton thoroughly before such a race? Lord Belfast, once he was recovered enough to speak, informed some of his friends that his staff had thoroughly repaired, cleaned, and gone over the phaeton before the race. There is no explanation for the wheel simply removing itself... unless it is, of course, that Lord Anderton sent someone to make sure that it would do so." Clearing his throat, he shook his head to himself. "You stated that Lord Belfast is not present at the London Season. That is true. It is because he is too unwell to return to London. His injuries from the fall were severe."

Still trying to chase his doubts away, Phillip shook his head.

"I can hardly even countenance the suggestion that Lord Anderton was responsible. To do such a thing to a gentleman would be terrible indeed!"

Lord Marchmont lifted both hands.

"And as I have said, I cannot tell you that it was he who

did so. I have no proof, but my concerns about him remain the same. After all, what sort of gentleman would demand his winnings from a wager after his opponent was lying unconscious, bleeding, and broken?"

Phillip's jaw dropped open, unable to hide his concern any longer.

"You mean to say-?"

"Yes." Lord Marchmont scowled. "Lord Anderton demanded his winnings immediately thereafter from one of Lord Belfast's men and, upon receiving no favorable response, waited in Belfast's townhouse. I believe, the moment that Lord Belfast was conscious, Lord Anderton was there asking for his winnings to be given to him. *That* does not speak of a fine character. Not to me, at least."

Nodding, Phillip coupled his hands and looked across to where Lord Anderton was now sitting with some other gentlemen. They were all talking and laughing together, making it appear as though Lord Anderton was nothing but a jovial sort, who appreciated a little bit of fun when it came to placing bets and the like. Could it be that he had another motivation in suggesting such a thing to Phillip?

"Will you tell me about this wager?" Lord Marchmont lifted an eyebrow as Phillip shot him a quick glance. "I swear I shall not make any judgment. I speak only as your friend and with concern."

Taking a moment, Phillip considered, then nodded.

"It is foolishness," he began, aware of a gentle heat creeping up his neck. "There is apparently a Lady Allan-thorpe whom no gentleman has ever been able to pull into his arms. Her husband died some years ago and while she lingers in society, she shows no interest in cavorting with anyone." He did not seem to need to say anything more, for Lord Marchmont closed his eyes and let out a heavy sigh, clearly anticipating what the wager was to be. "It is to be nothing more than a kiss, however," Phillip finished quickly. "I am only to have one opportunity and Lord Anderton will be nearby to make certain that he witnesses whatever occurs."

"Lady Allanthorpe is one of the most well-respected widows in all of London." Lord Marchmont ran one hand over his face. "She has more than enough wealth to keep her satisfied for the rest of her days, although she is most generous with all that she has. I believe one of the local orphanages has benefited from her patronage and to embroil her in scandal would be utterly diabolical... especially if she is to be unaware of it." Another harsh breath rattled from him. "Did you not even consider this before accepting the wager?"

"I did not know who she was."

Phillip's excuse felt small and weak and as Lord Marchmont let out another exclamation, Phillip shrank low in his seat. Lord Marchmont had not said a single word to shame him, but Phillip felt the weight of it on his shoulders regardless. His excuse was a poor one. Yes, he ought to have been a good deal more considerate, a good deal more thoughtful over who it was he was expected to pull into his arms, rather than looking at this only as a wager between himself and Lord Anderton.

"You are a scoundrel indeed." Lord Marchmont growled, threw back his brandy, and then rose from his chair. "Excuse me. I think I shall take my leave now."

Phillip made to say something, but no words came. His eyes followed Lord Marchmont as his friend made his way across the room, noting that he did not go to leave White's. Rather, he sat down with another group of gentlemen, as though he could not stomach Phillip's company a moment longer.

Closing his eyes, Phillip accepted the heat of shame which began to flood through him. What had he done? The wager was made, and it was not as though he could pull away from it now. Yet, deep within him, the beginnings of regret began to grow... but it was all coming much too late.

CHAPTER THREE

*D*eborah smiled as conversation turned to Lord Coppinger, who was a close friend of Lady Almeria's. Her smile dimmed a little as Lady Almeria dropped her gaze, for it did not appear that her friend had any desire to speak of him. Lady Yardley was making the point that the gentleman ought to be introduced to those of Lady Almeria's friends yet unmarried, which included Deborah herself. Pausing, Deborah considered Lord Coppinger for a moment. Yes, he was handsome and appeared to be quite the gentleman but, given Lady Almeria's lack of enthusiasm, Deborah pushed away any eagerness within herself to become better acquainted with him. Perhaps, she considered, there was something more to the friendship between Lady Almeria and Lord Coppinger – something that, as yet, Lady Almeria had not considered.

"I have heard many people say that they are grateful to you for your warning about Lord Brookmire's return to London, Lady Yardley." It was Lady Elizabeth who spoke, but everyone else nodded their agreement. "He has done nothing as yet to declare himself a rogue, but I am certain that he will do so very soon."

At this, Deborah let out a snort of agreement which garnered her the attention of the others. Laughing, she shook her head before quickly explaining her reaction.

"It is only that I did not know of this gentleman, nor of his reputation before my mother spoke to me of him, and thereafter Lady Elizabeth did also. I had the unfortunate moment of being introduced to him against my desire. The gentleman appeared quite determined to make himself known to me, and given propriety's expectation, there was nothing Lady Elizabeth could do other than to introduce us."

Lady Yardley lifted an eyebrow.

"And did you find him to be *very* charming?"

Her ironic tone made everyone laugh and, as Lady Elizabeth giggled, Deborah shared a smile with her friend.

"I found him quite arrogant, to be truthful, though I will admit openly that he is very handsome. I can see why so many ladies might be drawn to him."

This was said with a slight shrug of her shoulders and no blush warming her cheeks. It was not an embarrassment to state that Lord Brookmire was handsome, for every other young lady in London seemed to think so and she had no doubt that her friends were of a similar mind.

"I believe that Miss Madeley spoke to him in a manner which he was most unaccustomed to." Again, Lady Elizabeth giggled and many of her friends smiled also. "He was most displeased with her. I am certain that he will not return to our company soon."

Lady Yardley laughed as Deborah smiled at her.

"I have every confidence that you were more than able to state quite directly that you did not wish to enjoy his company, Miss Madeley." Her smile faded a little. "Though I would urge you to be cautious. I do not know him particularly well, but gentlemen like Lord Brookmire are often inclined towards pride. If you have injured it, there is every chance that he will attempt to force his acquaintance upon you, even if you do not wish for it. He may try again, and may seek to encourage you to think well of him, despite your promise that you will not do so. He will see it as a victory."

Deborah nodded, taking Lady Yardley's warning with great seriousness.

"I have already promised my mother that I will not be seen either in prolonged conversation or dancing with him." She lifted both shoulders. "Not that such a thing is of any trial to me. Should Lord Brookmire try again, I have every intention of being just as forthright with him as I was the first time."

Lady Yardley nodded, but she did not smile. Her warning continued to linger in Deborah's mind as the conversation then floated to something else. Was Lord Brookmire truly as determined as that? Would he again seek her out, would he try to make her accept him? With a small smile, Deborah shook her head to herself. Try as he might, she was quite certain that she would never allow herself to be cajoled into accepting Lord Brookmire as a suitable acquaintance, nor even as a gentleman.

"Goodness, I am quite exhausted." Deborah laughed as she slipped her arm through Lord Cleverley's. "An excellent dance, Lord Cleverley."

The gentleman smiled down at her.

"It was very pleasing, Miss Madeley, and might I say, you are a remarkable dancer."

She giggled, a little surprised at her flush of warmth at his words.

"You may say so," she answered, softly. "I did enjoy my time dancing with you."

Lord Cleverley smiled and to her surprise, reached across to press her hand as it rested on his arm. Lord Cleverly was a tall, slim fellow whose features were not overly handsome, but whose eyes always sparkled when they talked and whose smile was always kind. This was the third time they had danced together most recently and, as she had done before, Deborah continued to enjoy his conversation.

"I wonder," Lord Cleverley continued after a moment, as their steps slowed. "Might you ever be willing to take a walk with me through the park, Miss Madeley? Or perhaps even a carriage ride? Of course, I should probably call upon you first, but I confess I find it difficult to have a prolonged conversation when the time to take tea is so short and, no doubt, you will be surrounded by a good many gentlemen all wishing to capture your conversation and attention for themselves."

Deborah laughed softly.

"I think that you consider me a little too highly."

"Indeed, I do not think so!" Lord Cleverley responded quickly. "I consider you a diamond or a flower that I should like to pluck before it is chosen by another." Her smile dropped, for she did not much like this explanation, only for Lord Cleverley to laugh somewhat brokenly and shake his head. "Forgive me, I am not particularly used to having to express myself in such a manner, and I am sure that I do not find the correct terms to compliment a lady. Please forgive me for my lack of sensibility in this. What I am attempting to say is that I find you most wonderful, and I should very much like to spend more time in your company... that is, if you should wish to do so also."

Deborah's lips curved upwards as he released her arm so that they could stand facing each other. She found Lord Cleverley rather endearing, particularly in his attempts to speak honestly of his desires as regarded their acquaintance.

"I thank you, Lord Cleverley, for your honesty." She smiled brightly. "It is very kind of you."

Lord Cleverley's lips lifted for a moment before dropping again, clearly still a little uncertain.

"Then will you accept me?"

"I shall accept your offer for a walk together in the park, certainly."

Deborah refused to permit herself to say more than that, for fear she would find herself drawn towards him when she was not certain that she wished to be.

I am still to find a gentleman to fall in love with and while Lord Cleverley is quite pleasing, such feelings take time to grow.

"I am delighted to hear it!"

Deborah laughed softly at his exuberance.

"Shall we say perhaps the day after tomorrow?"

Lord Cleverley grinned suddenly, his cheeks filling with color as he passed one hand over his forehead. Clearly this was had been more of a strain than Deborah had realized!

"I should like that very much, Miss Madeley." With another smile, he dropped his hand to his side. "The day after tomorrow. Yes, that would suit me very well."

"But have you not forgotten, Miss Madeley? You and I have an arrangement the day after tomorrow."

A deep voice broke into their conversation, immediately wiping the smile from Lord Cleverley's face and replacing it with a deep frown. Deborah swung around to see who was speaking to her in such a way, only for a deep and unsettling anger to bubble up from the pit of her stomach, flooding right through her.

"Do please ignore Lord Brookmire." She rolled her eyes as Lord Cleverley's frown continued to grow. "He jests, Lord Cleverley. I am certain that you will understand that a lady of my standing would never permit herself to be caught by a gentleman with such a reputation as Lord Brookmire holds."

The frown was immediately wiped from Lord Cleverley's face.

"Ah. Of course. I quite understand."

He lifted his chin a little and folded his arms across his chest before coming to stand a little closer to Deborah's side; a show of strength, perhaps, against Lord Brookmire's arrogance.

"Why is it that you will accept Lord Cleverley's company, but you will not tolerate even a moment of mine?"

Deborah tapped her foot in impatience, letting out a long and heavy sigh.

"Are we truly to have the same discussion again, Lord Brookmire? You know full well my reasons and, therefore, it will come as no surprise to you that I have every intention of extricating myself from this conversation almost immediately."

Lord Brookmire joined her in her sighs by letting out a long one of his own, and looking upwards as though pleading to heaven for some sort of aid.

"But should not a gentleman ever be offered a second chance? Another opportunity to prove himself to a lady?"

Deborah bit her lip before she could answer. The gentleman was once more goading her, and she had no time for him – but it seemed the only way in which she could prove that was to remain silent.

"I take it from your silence that you will not offer me such an opportunity."

Turning her head, Deborah returned her gaze to Lord Cleverley.

"Might you return me to my mother, Lord Cleverley?" she asked softly. "I have no concern as regards *your* company, but I am very aware that she will find our present company rather displeasing."

Lord Brookmire only chortled, but Lord Cleverley immediately nodded.

"I should be more than glad to do so." With a firm look towards Lord Brookmire, he turned away from him. "Do excuse us."

Deborah too offered a prim but short smile to Lord Brookmire and turned away, only for him to suddenly grasp her hand and tug her gently back. She made to respond fiercely, to demand to know where such audacity came from, only for her words to steal themselves away as her breath lodged itself in her chest. Something like fire erupted within her core, and as she looked into Lord Brookmire's face, a dull ache formed even lower in her belly. He was saying something, grinning at her, but she could not seem to hear him. Her hand was still in his and it was only when Lord Cleverley touched her arm that she pulled it sharply away from Lord Brookmire's grasp. Her extraordinary reaction to his nearness had her dumbfounded, and with a slight lift of her chin, she turned away from him directly, while finding herself deeply troubled at how strangely she had responded.

"I can only apologize." Lord Cleverley shook his head as Deborah attempted to compose herself. "I should have taken you away from Lord Brookmire a good deal more quickly than I did. You are not the only one aware of his reputation. I do hope that your mother will not be displeased at our lingering."

Deborah forced a quick smile.

"I do not think that you need have any concern, Lord Cleverley," she told him quickly. "Instead, my mother will simply be pleased that you took me away from him. I am grateful to you for doing so without hesitation."

Lord Cleverley blinked for a moment, then smiled and nodded, seeming relieved at her reassurance. Within only a few moments, they were standing beside Lady Prescott again, and Deborah let out a slow yet unobtrusive breath.

"I saw Lord Brookmire attempt to speak with you again." Lady Prescott turned to smile brilliantly up into Lord Cleverley's face. "And I also observed how quickly you removed my daughter from his presence. I am very grateful to you, Lord Cleverley."

The gentleman inclined his head.

"I only wish that I had done so a good deal more quickly," he replied, as Deborah looked from one to the other, trying to remove the unsettling feelings as regarded Lord Brookmire from within herself. With a deep breath, she set her shoulders in an attempt to regain the composure she had been so certain she had fully within her control... right up until the moment Lord Brookmire had taken her hand.

"Deborah?" Blinking rapidly, she looked at her mother, seeing the slightly questioning look. "What was it Lord Brookmire spoke to you about?"

A slight flush came into Deborah's cheeks.

"Very little of consequence." She shook her head. "If you can believe it, he was attempting to ingratiate himself, in the hope that I would succumb to his charms." Allowing herself a small exclamation of disapproval, she sighed. "It appears as though his pride is a little injured, since I have not warmed to him as so many others have done."

Lord Cleverley nodded fervently.

"Might I suggest that he is unused to having anyone reject him so fervently?" He sent her a warm smile. "I admire your confidence in speaking with him so firmly."

Deborah smiled briefly. "Thank you again for taking me from him."

It was the only thing she could think to say, given how her mind was in torment over her strange reaction to Lord Brookmire's touch. Again, her mother praised Lord Cleverley, and after a few moments, he excused himself, telling Deborah upon departure that he looked forward to dancing with her again soon. Deborah smiled and curtsied, then watched as Lord Cleverley moved away from her side in search of the next young lady he should dance with. Her eyes fixed themselves on him, waiting for a slight pang of jealousy or hint of envy that he should be standing up with someone else... but none came. It was the most extraordinary thing, for if she was as delighted with Lord Cleverley as she knew she was, and if he was eager to call upon her, ought she not to feel something?

"Lord Cleverley is a very excellent sort." Lady Prescott cast a considering eye over Deborah's features. "He does appear a little taken with you."

Deborah looked back at her.

"He has asked if I will walk with him in the park in two days' time."

Her mother did not respond with a great exclamation of pleasure, nor did she gasp in evident delight. Instead, she simply waited for Deborah to continue and, hearing the silent question, Deborah spread out both hands.

"Of course I accepted him. He is, as you yourself said, an excellent gentleman."

Lady Prescott smiled.

"He certainly is and would be an ideal match, but only if you would be contented with him. This is not something that you must hurry into, Deborah. This is a moment in your life where you must take your time and consider all that must be done, as well as your feelings towards the gentleman, before you accept even a request of courtship."

Even as she murmured her agreement, Deborah found her gaze falling upon none other than Lord Brookmire. He was walking alongside another gentleman, their heads close together, his hands clasped tightly behind his back. What they were discussing, she did not know but, all the same, her heart quickened a little. She could not help but recall all she had felt when Lord Brookmire had taken her hand. Frustration twined with the heat that still coiled through her as she pulled her eyes away from him. It was most confounding. Why should she react so strongly to Lord Brookmire, but feel very little when it came to Lord Cleverley – a gentleman who was much more suitable for her, and certainly more respectable than Lord Brookmire could ever be?

It was the shock of it, she told herself silently, *the shock of having him take my hand in such a demanding manner.*

Nodding slowly to herself, Deborah took in a deep breath and then released it slowly. This was the only possible explanation for her response, and it was one that she was going to force herself to accept regardless of the questions it brought up within her. She turned her thoughts to an entirely different matter, wondering whether Lady Almeria had found any particular gentleman to dance with that evening, or whether she might make her introductions of Lord Coppinger to another one of their friends. Time and again, her thoughts sought to twist themselves back to Lord Brookmire and her fiery response to his nearness, but with an effort she kept consideration of him away. He was the last person she wanted to think about, and whether or not it took her all of her strength, she was determined not to do so... and, in addition, she would be sure to make certain that Lord Brookmire never touched her again.

CHAPTER FOUR

"*D*o you see her?"

Phillip nodded. His conversation with Miss Madeley was still lingering in his mind, and try as he might, he could not remove her face from his thoughts yet again. She was the most infuriating young lady of his acquaintance and therefore, why he had even stopped to speak with her, he could not say. The distraction of Lady Allanthorpe, and even the company of Lord Anderton was preferable to standing alone and thinking of Miss Madeley.

"Aha! I *am* acquainted with the lady, in fact." Catching sight of Lady Allanthorpe as Lord Anderton indicated her, he took her in. She was a petite lady who was nowhere near her dotage, with sparkling brown eyes and reddish brown hair, which was curled into ringlets. He found himself smiling. It would not take any great difficulty on his part to kiss a lady with such resplendent features as she, he was sure of it. "I am sure that I will be able to persuade her to dance with me and, thereafter, step out into the night air."

Lord Anderton shook his head.

"I do not think that she will step out of doors with you.

She is not inclined to the company of gentlemen, as I have already informed you. You will have to watch for her making her way there and, once outside, take your opportunity."

Phillip sent a considered look toward Lord Anderton.

"You appear to be very eager for me to succeed here."

Lord Anderton immediately snorted with evident laughter.

"No, indeed, I am eager to see you fail," he remarked, digging his elbow into Phillip's ribs. "I give you the opportunity only, not because I am eager to see you succeed, but only because I am eager to gain my winnings from you, as soon as possible!"

"Is that so?"

Phillip considered, looking at Lord Anderton again, doubting the man's words, but Lord Anderton only chuckled. He was a gentleman who always seemed to find something mirthful, Phillip considered. In fact, all Lord Anderton appeared to do was laugh, though whether or not it was currently at Phillip's expense, he could not say for certain.

"What do you think you should do?" Lord Anderton tilted his head, but his eyes remained on the lady in front of them. "As I have said, your best opportunity might be to take her when she is out of doors. Then again, you may wish to attempt to kiss her in the shadows of the ballroom, but-"

"No, I do not think that it would be a wise idea to attempt to do so here."

Phillip shook his head, his teeth worrying at the edge of his lip. Whether Lord Anderton realized it or not, his suggestion was a wise one. It would *not* be a good idea to attempt to kiss Lady Allanthorpe here in the ballroom, for not only would she most likely push him away, given that they would be in public, he was also a little concerned as regarded her reputation. He did not want her to be touched by scandal. Yes, he was something of a rogue, certainly, but then again, in this situation, he could not simply forget about the reputation of the lady. There was certainly no desire for him to damage Lady Allanthorpe's standing amongst London society, simply because of Lord Anderton's wager – Lord Marchmont had convinced him enough of that!

"Then you will go out of doors?" Lord Anderton chuckled, and Phillip's teeth clenched hard together at the sound. He severely regretted taking on this wager with Lord Anderton now, given not only how irritating the man could be, but also how uncertain he felt about it all. Yes, he had every intention of winning it and held every confidence he would do so, but all the same, since Lord Marchmont's warning, Phillip had become a trifle more concerned.

"Dance with her." Lord Anderton wiggled his eyebrows. "I shall dance with her thereafter and, no doubt, after two such dances, she will be quite fatigued and will be agreeable to the suggestion to take the air. I think that situation would suit you very well."

Again, Phillip frowned, finding that Lord Anderton's suggestion was, for the second time, a good one while at the same time, beginning to question why the gentleman was being so helpful. It was very odd indeed. Unless it was simply that Lord Anderton had every belief that he would win the wager, in which case, he might simply be eager for his winnings, as he had said. But all the same, there was a great deal of doubt in Phillip's heart. Doubt which he could not push aside.

"I shall sign her dance card at the very least! Come!"

Without waiting for Phillip's agreement, Lord

Anderton made his way directly to the lady and the companions she spoke with. Blinking, Phillip hesitated, wondering whether or not he ought to follow Lord Anderton or stand a little further back and wait for an opportunity when Lord Anderton was *not* speaking with her, only to realize that, if he did not speak with her now, he might very well find her dances already taken when he approached her later in the evening.

With reluctance, he made his way after Lord Anderton, making certain to amble towards the group of ladies as though he had no real intention of making his way there.

"Ah, Lord Brookmire!" Lord Anderton gestured to him, and Phillip smiled quickly. He did not look at Lady Allanthorpe immediately, but quickly turned his attention to the other ladies, first to Lady Essington. She spoke with him, as did Lady Harrogate, and then, Phillip turned his attention to Lady Allanthorpe at last. It was, of course, his way of making certain that he did not make too much of her presence. The last thing he wanted was for her to think that he was interested in her company, for fear that she would then seek to push him away before he had even had the opportunity to get close enough to win the wager.

"It is a very pleasant evening, is it not."

Phillip smiled widely, then looked around at each of the ladies.

"It is." Lady Harrogate replied. "And have you both been dancing?"

Her gaze swept over Phillip quickly before being pulled away. Clearly, she knew of his reputation and was not particularly inclined to speak with him.

Lord Anderton chortled.

"Certainly, I have, but I am afraid that I am not as sought after as Lord Brookmire."

He shot Phillip a glance and a grin, but Phillip merely shrugged, not taking the opportunity which Lord Anderton was giving him. He did not want to make himself too obvious.

"And have you been enjoying watching the dancing?" he asked Lady Essington, again keeping his attention from Lady Allanthorpe. The lady stated that yes, she had thus far had the most enjoyable evening but was mostly concerned with her daughter, who, while being courted by a gentleman of particular note, was not yet betrothed. Lady Harrogate murmured something about her own daughter, and Phillip listened as carefully as he could, smiling first at Lady Essington and thereafter turning his attention to Lady Allanthorpe again.

"And you, Lady Allanthorpe, have you been enjoying the evening?"

The lady's expression was somewhat surprising. Given his reputation, he had expected her to either look away from him entirely, or to give him only the briefest of glances, as Lady Harrogate had done. The fact that she looked at him so directly was a little unexpected – as was her brief smile.

"I do find such social occasions to be most pleasing, although that is usually dependent on the company."

Her eyebrow lifted just a little, a tiny smile at one corner of her mouth. Clearing his throat, Phillip, somewhat abashed, put both hands behind his back. Evidently, it was all too obvious that Lady Allanthorpe knew precisely who he was and the details of his reputation.

"I am certain that you have excellent company in Lady Harrogate and Lady Essington." She laughed softly and Phillip did not miss the broad, delighted smile which crossed Lord Anderton's face. Why such a smile should be, he was not certain. Did the gentleman know that Phillip would gain his opportunity with Lady Allanthorpe? And if there was an opportunity for him, then what exactly would happen thereafter? For a moment he began to fear that Lord Anderton had spoken to Lady Allanthorpe in advance of this, that they had arranged the whole situation together so that he would not succeed. Lady Allanthorpe, perhaps, knew exactly what was about to happen, meaning that she and Lord Anderton together had concocted this scheme simply to gain some extra coin for Lord Anderton. Swallowing hard, he tried to smile and pushed his thoughts away. "Have you danced very much this evening, Lady Allanthorpe?"

Her eyebrows dropped back into position.

"No, I have not. However, I am not certain that I wish to this evening, for I have had a great deal of enjoyment in speaking with my friends, and perhaps a dance would pull me away from their fine company."

Phillip nodded.

"I quite understand but, should you change your mind, I would be very happy indeed to stand up with you."

"As would I," Lord Anderton added quickly, as though it were an afterthought. "And indeed, you also, Lady Essington if you would like to dance? And you, Lady-"

"No, no. Not in the least." Lady Harrogate shook her head, holding up one hand in Lord Anderton's direction, as if to push him back. "I certainly have no intention of dancing this evening. I am quite contented to be watching my daughter."

"As am I." Lady Essington laughed softly and shook her head "So you may take that hopeful glint out of your eye, Lord Anderton, for I shall not be dancing either. As I have said, I am continuously watching over my daughter, as Lady Harrogate is over hers. I should not like her to become diverted nor the gentleman who is courting her to become distracted by someone else, either."

A heavy sigh slipped from Lord Anderton's throat.

"Then it seems as though you are our only hope, Lady Allanthorpe." He spread out both hands as Phillip allowed himself a small smile. "Will you also reject us? Will you also turn your back and refuse to step out with either of us?"

Lady Allanthorpe paused for a moment, then smiled.

"You paint a very despondent picture, Lord Anderton. So certainly, I will step out with you."

She held out her dance card and Phillip immediately moved to snatch it from Lord Anderton's fingers, chuckling as he did so. After all, his reputation was one of a scoundrel, so why should he not act the part?

"If you are to dance with Lord Anderton, then I am certain that you will dance with me also." He grinned at the lady. "You cannot accept him and refuse me. I should be broken-hearted!"

Lady Allanthorpe put both hands on her hips, her chin lifting.

"But he has not the reputation you hold."

Phillip chuckled, finding himself falling back into that familiar teasing manner he so often used whenever he was talking to a lady.

"That may be true, but he is not as good a dancer as I."

At this, Lady Allanthorpe gave such a laugh that Phillip knew for certain that she was about to assent, and therefore he immediately looked down at the dances. Seeing there were two free, coming one after the next, he wrote his name down for the quadrille and then handed the card to Lord Anderton, seeing the gentleman tilt his head a little before writing his name for the country dance. The suggestion that Lord Anderton had made had been followed exactly.

"I do feel as though I have been a little compelled into this situation." Lady Allanthorpe accepted the dance card back from Lord Anderton with a gracious smile. "It is not often that I dance at any ball, so you both must think yourselves to be very fortunate indeed."

Phillip replied only with a bow, whilst Lord Anderton assured her that yes, they did feel very lucky to be able to stand up with her. As they both stepped away, Phillip could not help but cast a glance over his shoulder. Lady Allanthorpe was beautiful, yet respectable and a very pleasing lady. He had not anticipated that she would be so pleasant to speak with, and there were now the first strains of guilt in his heart that he would now be seeking to do something both improper and forward to such a pleasant woman. But yet the wager was made, and therefore there was nothing he could do now but act upon it.

"I shall lead her out to the gardens once our dance is at an end." Lord Anderton nudged him again. "You must be ready."

Nodding, Phillip turned his gaze away from Lady Allanthorpe.

"Be assured that I will be more than prepared. The wager will be won this evening in *my* favor, Lord Anderton. You can be sure of that."

PHILLIP MOVED QUICKLY, his eyes on Lord Anderton and Lady Allanthorpe. A small crowd pressed between himself and the gentleman, but he was still able to keep him in sight. His heartbeat sped up rather quickly, a surge of energy running through his frame. Something held him back, slowing his steps, telling him to forget the wager – and into his mind came the warnings of Lord Marchmont.

He knew that what he was about to do was not right. He knew that it was not wise, but pride would not allow him to pull back. He either did what he had wagered to do, certain that he would gain a great deal of coin from Lord Anderton - money which he did not necessarily need, but which he wished for nonetheless- or did not even attempt to tug Lady Allanthorpe into his arms.

The latter option would mean that he would lose the wager immediately, for Lord Anderton would win by default. He would be forced to hand over his coin to Lord Anderton, having never had the opportunity to prove himself. Should he do so then, no doubt, Lord Anderton would tell all of his acquaintances precisely what had happened. Phillip would be mocked, laughed at, and even scorned for, of a certainty, Lord Anderton would speak with glee over the fact that the scoundrel who was Lord Brookmire had stepped back from this challenge - and that was something which Phillip had no desire to be faced with. Straightening his shoulders, he followed Lord Anderton and Lady Allanthorpe out into the dark evening. The gardens were well lit, but there were plenty of shadowy places for him to linger should he desire it.

He saw Lord Anderton looking at him over his shoulder, and Phillip merely nodded, watching carefully as Lord Anderton let go of the arm of the lady. The gentleman wandered a little to the left and the lady followed him, stepping away from the path and under a few trees – and out of sight of the other guests. It was a little surprising to Phillip that Lady Allanthorpe would be so indiscreet, particularly after what Lord Anderton had told him about her... but then again, mayhap Lord Anderton had embellished that some-what. Pushing aside his concerns, Phillip hurried forward until he came upon the lady. Lord Anderton laughed loudly, turned swiftly, and stepped away. A small exclama-tion of surprise at Lord Anderton's behavior came from the lady, only for Phillip to step closer, sweeping his arms around Lady Allanthorpe's waist and lowering his head.

This was the moment when he would either prove himself to be just as was believed – a scoundrel and one who could steal a kiss from any lady, should he wish it – or when he would fail. Would Lady Allanthorpe pull back from him, slap him hard across the face, and leave Lord Anderton to win the wager?

The shock of his actions had her first instinct held back for, initially, she remained frozen and fixed in his arms. Thereafter, however, she began to soften and much to Phillip's surprise, leaned closer towards him. Her hands went to his chest, then pushed up to his shoulders whilst he wrapped his arms a little more around her so that she was pulled tight against him. When it was *she* who angled her head, Phillip jolted in astonishment at her boldness, before breaking the kiss. Something was warning him that all was not well. He had been told by Lord Marchmont *and* by Lord Anderton that Lady Allanthorpe was someone who would pull back from a gentleman, who would not want to be drawn into his embrace, and now here she was, behaving as though she had long desired such a kiss from him. How could such a thing be? He could not understand it.

"Excuse me."

Phillip cleared his throat, feeling somewhat abashed and not at all certain of what he ought to do next. Peering at the lady in the flickering darkness, he caught his breath when she reached for him again, one hand out to catch the lapel of his jacket.

Phillip's alarm grew like a whirlwind. Something was clearly wrong, yet he could not place what it was. This was not how he had anticipated Lady Allanthorpe would act, and Lord Anderton would surely not have placed such a wager if he had expected Lady Allanthorpe to be so willing to accept Phillip.

"Lady... Lady Allanthorpe?"

Someone chuckled near him, and Phillip rolled his eyes, just as Lord Anderton's hand fell on his shoulder.

"Lady Allanthorpe?"

The lady he had been kissing only a moment ago repeated her name, sounding rather astonished as if she had not expected him to say her name with such clarity. Before Phillip could ask her anything more, Lord Anderton was slapping him on the back and laughing aloud.

"My hearty congratulations. It appears as though you have won our wager."

Lord Anderton's voice was loud and booming and, before Phillip could reply, the lady in question let out such a gasp of either horror or dismay, that Phillip was startled at her response. Surely a lady such as Lady Allanthorpe, who was widowed and knew all too well of his reputation, would not be surprised that he had done something as stupid as to accept a wager from Lord Anderton over kissing a lady. There was no time to speak of it, for the lady let out what sounded like a sob before hurrying away, leaving guilt to wind its way slowly through Phillip's veins.

His head dropped, his eyes squeezing closed as his stomach began to swirl this way and that. He felt no plea-sure in winning the wager, and immediately made to go after her, only to be held back by Lord Anderton's surprisingly strong grasp. Frustrated, he looked sharply at the man.

"The lady is upset."

Lord Anderton snorted and shrugged his shoulders, finally lifting his hand from Phillip's shoulder.

"What care you for that? You must have expected it! Surely you did not think that Lady Allanthorpe would be pleased that you stole a kiss from her, even if it was done in the very dark recesses of the gardens?"

Phillip rubbed one hand over his eyes, still feeling distinctly uncomfortable about what had just taken place.

"But you have won the wager." Lord Anderton shook his head and turned to walk back towards the path with Phillip following after him. "I suppose I should not have placed a wager with a gentleman with your reputation, but I could not help but try. I wanted to see if you could be proven wrong, but alas, it seems in this case you shall win a great deal of money from me."

Phillip licked his lips. He wanted very much to say that he cared nothing for the money, that the wager ought never to have been undertaken, and that he deeply regretted all which had taken place, but instead he said nothing. Lord Anderton continued to speak about some matter or other, but Phillip barely listened. Instead, the warnings from Lord Marchmont about Lord Anderton continually rang in his mind. Even though he had won the wager, his thoughts were even louder, as though somehow, deep within him, he knew that this matter was not entirely resolved. There was a shadow over him now, a threat of something more to come, though what it was waiting for him, Phillip could not know. All he could do was wait for it to fall upon his shoulders and crush him where he lay.

CHAPTER FIVE

"I do wonder if Lord Brookmire will be present this evening."

Catching the glint in her friend's gaze, Deborah rolled her eyes.

"I know very well that you are teasing me. I care very little as to whether or not Lord Brookmire is present. I have no time for him whatsoever, as you are all too aware."

Lady Elizabeth chuckled.

"Though I do wonder whether he will attempt to place himself in your company regardless," she suggested, the gleam in her eye remaining. "I look forward to hearing what you have to say to him, should he try to do so."

At this, Deborah grinned, her cheeks glowing with sudden laughter.

"He might, but should he dare, I have prepared myself," she acknowledged with a giggle. "Not only this morning but also before the ball, I looked at myself in the mirror and recited what I might say to Lord Brookmire should he approach. You need not worry, my dear friend. I am very well prepared."

At this, Lady Elizabeth's eyes twinkled as she laughed softly.

"Part of me is almost hopeful that he will, in fact, come to your company, simply so that I might hear what you say to him."

The two friends laughed together and Lady Elizabeth slipped her arm through Deborah's so that they might walk together around the ballroom. Their mothers were both in conversation and had allowed the two friends to promenade together around the ballroom under the strict promise that they would return to them directly thereafter. The ball was a little quieter than usual, for Lord Balfour had only invited a select number of guests, but Deborah was glad of it. Since it was a little less busy, it might afford her opportunities to further her acquaintance with particular gentlemen... including Lord Cleverley.

"Did you enjoy your time with Lord Cleverley?" Her friend tilted her head as though she knew precisely who had been in Deborah's mind "You have not spoken much of him nor of your walk together."

Deborah smiled quickly as if she were suddenly determined to make certain her friend believed that the afternoon had gone very well, although why she had forgotten to speak of it, she could not say. Surely, if she had been thrilled with his company, she would have been eager to speak of her time with him to her friend, without Lady Elizabeth first prompting her? Pushing the troubling thought aside, she offered her smile to her friend.

"Yes, of course. It was a most enjoyable afternoon. He is a very fine fellow and I find him easy to converse with." Catching Lady Elizabeth's questioning look, Deborah shrugged. "I cannot say as yet if I shall fall in love with him, however. I do find him very amiable as I have said, but I am still waiting for any particular feelings to develop."

"Which may come in time," her friend replied as Deborah nodded in agreement. "It is good that you are being cautious. I am certain that, should a gentleman such as Lord Cleverley look at me in the way he looks at you, I would find myself quite in love with him the very next moment!"

Laughing softly, Deborah shook her head.

"I do not think that he looks at me in any particular way. Besides which he is calling upon other young ladies also."

Lady Elizabeth tilted her head.

"But he has not asked any other young lady for a walk in the park." Her eyes glowed gently. "I am sure that Lord Cleverley might consider you only, if you offered him even the smallest encouragement."

There was a little uncertainty in Deborah's mind as to whether or not she wished to give Lord Cleverley an indication that she might be inclined towards him alone, and thus she remained silent. Lady Elizabeth, being a very tactful sort of person, and clearly aware that Deborah was giving the matter a good deal of consideration, stayed quiet also. Thus, they continued their promenade around the ballroom and Deborah opened her mouth to say something more, only to be apprehended by a strong hand on her wrist.

Immediately, her arm dropped from that of Lady Elizabeth and she turned around sharply, only for Lord Brookmire's face to flood her view. With great fury burning through her veins, she shook off his hand then spun away from him.

"Let us make our way directly back towards our mothers," she hissed to Lady Elizabeth, ignoring Lord Brookmire, and beginning to stride across the room.

To her utter shock, however, Lord Brookmire's hand grasped hers once more, and even more horrifying, he pulled her back towards the shadows at the edge of the room. Lady Elizabeth let out some sort of exclamation, but Lord Brookmire simply ignored it. His voice was quiet, a low whisper hissing words towards her, but such was her shock, Deborah could barely hear him. Her response to his nearness was more than overwhelming, and the more she looked at him, the longer he held her hand in his, the more she felt it. Her heart was pounding hard in her chest, blood boiling, but the anger she had felt was already fading away. Every part of her skin tingled in a most disconcerting manner and, try as she might, she could not speak a word. Her breath lodged itself deep within her and she could only take short, sharp breaths as she looked back into his eyes. It was both frustrating and deeply irritating, for she certainly did not want to feel this way, but her heart seemed to betray her regardless.

"You must help me."

Lord Brookmire's hiss was low, and Deborah frowned, trying to understand what it was he spoke of, whilst regaining her own composure.

"Unhand her."

Lady Elizabeth's demand was what brought Deborah back to herself and, looking down at her hand, she saw her fingers were wound through Lord Brookmire's. With a gasp of shock, she pulled her hand away, relieved now that they were in the shadows at the side of the ballroom rather than anywhere near the center of the room. Her next look was to the other side of the ballroom where her mother and Lady Longford still stood but thankfully, the two were deep in conversation and had not seen a single thing. Thus far it seemed her reputation was quite safe and without even a hint of stain.

"You *must* help me, I beg of you!"

Again, Lord Brookmire's hand wrapped around her wrist, forcing Deborah's gaze back towards him.

"I think that you are mistaking me for someone else, Lord Brookmire," Deborah responded, keeping her voice low and trying to tug her hand away again, only to find that she lacked either the strength or the willingness to do so. Was there something about her that *wanted* him to take her hand? Something which desired his nearness? She took a moment to steady herself again and looked directly into Lord Brookmire's face. What she saw there, however, was most astonishing. Lord Brookmire's eyes were wide, his face very pale for there was not even a hint of color in his features. His usually sparkling eyes were faded to a dull green and his jaw set tight. For a moment she wavered, only to find the strength to take her hand away again and do so with a jerk. "I am *not* accustomed to gentlemen being as forward as you have been, Lord Brookmire. I have already made my position quite clear and-"

"I am very well aware of that, but yet I must beg for your help."

Lord Brookmire took a step closer and suddenly, all of Deborah's breath left her body as she gazed up into his eyes. His nearness was deeply transfixing and, despite her desire to stay far from him, despite her promise to both herself, and to her mother, that she would never linger in his company, she found herself doing precisely that. Lady Elizabeth was whispering something in harsh tones, but Deborah could not pay her heed. In fact, she could not make out a single word and instead, allowed herself to study Lord Brookmire's expression. His eyes roved around her face, an unspoken plea there which she could almost feel, deep within herself. Silently, he was begging her to listen to him, desperate for an opportunity to explain whatever it was that he was speaking of.

Or am I nothing but a fool?

Her eyes closed.

"Surely this is a ploy, Lord Brookmire." She let out a long breath, opening her eyes to see him shake his head fervently. *I ought not to trust him.* "I have been unwilling to countenance your company, and thus you are now attempting to find a way to force it upon me. Is that not so?"

Her lips pressed tightly together, and she was angry at herself for being so easily manipulated but, again, Lord Brookmire's hand found hers.

"It is not." Again, he stepped a little closer and, as her eyes danced down his frame, she caught sight of how tightly his hand was clenched. "I have been betrayed, I have been blackmailed, and it has all been achieved by taking advantage of my foolishness. I have been thinking of ways to extricate myself, only to realize that I have none. However, I then was reminded of the London Ledger, of how certain things were printed within it, and I can only pray that either yourself or Lady Yardley might be able to aid me in this. I am not known to her and wanted to ask if you would introduce me, for I have no other recourse. If I am left to face my situation alone - a situation which I will confess to be entirely my fault - then I will be ruined and...." Swallowing, he stopped for a moment, and Deborah took a breath, a little overwhelmed by how much he had disclosed to her in a short space of time. "I will be ruined," he said again, a good deal more quietly this time as his head hung forward "And not only myself, but a young lady. A young lady who has done nothing other than find herself betrayed by a gentleman she thought to trust. It is for her sake – and the sake of others – that I come to you." Taking a breath, he looked back at her steadily, his face still very pale indeed. "It is for his own ends and for his gains that the man who black-mails me does this, and therefore I am quite at a loss as to what to do. I fear that he will continually place this guilt upon me until I am quite ruined – and the lady also – and will, no doubt, take great pleasure in it also."

Her heart ached as Deborah waited for a response to come to her, a response which she would fling in Lord Brookmire's face, telling him that she had no desire to be anywhere near him, that she did not believe a single word of his account and that she certainly had no intention of wasting her time with his difficulties... only for those words to fade away. There was something about him that was different, something in his expression that demanded she believe him. It was most extraordinary, for everything within her told her that she would be foolish to accept even a single word that he said. But yet, despite such an aware-ness, her head ended up falling into a nod and, instantly, Lord Brookmire's eyes immediately closed.

"I..."

She had no ability to say it, so she nodded again.

"You will help me then."

There was a slight tremble to his voice, which had Deborah's eyebrows lifting and she shared a look with Lady Elizabeth, who, in the interim, had gone quite silent. It appeared that she also was both astonished and somewhat confused by Lord Brookmire's words, given the line which had formed between her brows. Her feelings corresponded precisely with all that Deborah herself held within herself.

"I do not say that I will help you, only that I will speak

with Lady Yardley for you." Deborah took a step back, making sure to stand closer to Lady Elizabeth and away from Lord Brookmire, silently praying that her mother had remained unobservant. The last thing she wished for was her mother to march across the ballroom and remove Lord Brookmire from her company, for that in itself would cause something of a scene! "You are not a gentleman whom I ought to trust."

Lord Brookmire lowered his head.

"I am well aware of that. Trust is not something that I demand from you, Miss Madeley. If it were, then you would find me at your feet, determined that I would gain what I desired from you in any way possible - but that is not the case, I can assure you. I want nothing from you other than to beg of you to speak to Lady Yardley and, thereafter, introduce me to her, should she be willing. I deserve none of this, of course. I know that my behavior has been utterly despicable - both last Season and this - but I cannot help but seek aid. No doubt, you will say that this dark situation is a consequence of my own choices, my trials due to my own foolishness, and I will readily accept that from you. As I have said, however, I have no desire for this young lady to be injured further than she already has been. Lord Anderton was cruel to her, as he has been cruel to me, and I am only regretful that I ever believed him."

None of this made any sense to Deborah, and she let out a slow breath, again looking to her companion, who still remained entirely silent.

"I do not comprehend anything of what you have said." Spreading out both hands as Lord Brookmire groaned and passed one hand over his eyes, she tipped her head gently. "However I can speak to Lady Yardley and ask if she is willing to be introduced to you. I will also state that you seek her aid and the aid of 'The London Ledger' in whatever situation you face."

Lord Brookmire nodded.

"That would be of the greatest assistance, Miss Madeley."

Deborah took a breath.

"Then I will speak with her now." Looking around the room, seeking to locate Lady Yardley, she caught her mother's glance, and winced, realizing that her mother would be wondering why she had not returned as yet. "You may follow us, Lord Brookmire but stay a short distance away." Taking Lady Elizabeth's arm, she gave him the smallest of smiles. "We must first go to my mother so that she is aware that I have returned to her side. I shall ask then to go to stand with Lady Yardley for a time and, when I have spoken with her, I shall indicate whether or not you are welcome. I warn you, however," she continued, a slight fear rising in her mind, a fear that he would turn around and, with a broad smile, declare that he had somehow managed a victory when it came to their previously cold acquaintance. "Lady Yardley is not as easily persuaded as I am and, mayhap, I am being foolish in this." She lifted a shoulder. "Mayhap you wish to declare it a victory that you and I have become a little better acquainted. Or perhaps it is that you will not speak with Lady Yardley at all but will instead simply laugh at me from across the room for believing your portrayal of a desperate man."

Lord Brookmire moved so close to her, there was barely a handspan between them. The scent of pine assailed her and Deborah's breath hitched, fresh warmth curling up like smoke from the pit of her stomach. His nearness to her was both overpowering and horrifying at the same time. Why was she responding to this gentleman in such a manner? He was a scoundrel, and she certainly did not trust him. Why should his nearness rob her of speech?

"I assure you that I shall do none of that." Lord Brookmire's hands now found hers and he squeezed her hands gently, sending a tremor up through her frame. "You will not find your trust in me misplaced."

Deborah, gathering herself, laughed and slid her hands from his.

"I think you will find, Lord Brookmire, that I do not trust you at all," she replied acerbically. "You may end up speaking with Lady Yardley, but I will have very little interest in whatever it is you have to say. I can assure you that, if Lady Yardley can aid you, then she will do so - but for my part, I do not think that we shall have any need to linger in conversation, nor in company. Do excuse me."

Aware that her words did not match the odd sense of longing which now swept through her as she left his side, she kept her head held high as she walked away. The desire to return to his company, the flicker of interest in hearing more of his situation and his explanation for his circumstances, grew with every step she took away from him. The two friends walked in silence as they made their way back towards their respective mothers, but Deborah's mind was so filled with heavy thoughts, she did not take in anything else which swept all around her.

This was a most extraordinary circumstance for, only some minutes ago, she had been saying to Lady Elizabeth that she had no intention of allowing Lord Brookmire anywhere near her and had been prepared with a set down should he attempt to approach her. Instead, she was now helping Lord Brookmire with a difficult circumstance - one he admitted he had brought upon himself. Has he truly had such a change of heart? Or could it be that Lord Brookmire's presence affected her more than she wanted to admit, even to herself?

CHAPTER SIX

*P*hillip pushed one hand through his hair, then the other. Pacing backward and forward at the edge of the ballroom, he continually slid glances towards Miss Madeley as she spoke to Lady Yardley. Thus far, this evening had been a complete disaster and, given what he had discovered, he now found himself in a situation where he had very few people to whom he could turn. When his thoughts had turned to Lady Yardley, he had gone hot all over with faint relief. Lady Yardley wrote 'The London Ledger' and therefore, she knew a great deal about society and those within it. Surely there was something she might be able to do to help him?

But only if she will speak with me.

Frustrated, he dropped his head, silently cursing himself for listening to Lord Anderton in the first place, and for refusing to listen to his inclinations, his doubts, and indeed to Lord Marchmont.

"You look particularly energetic this evening."

Lord Marchmont sent a broad smile towards Phillip,

who then winced as his friend's jovial tone grated against the angst which ran through him.

"I should have listened to you, Marchmont." Continuing his pacing, Phillip looked first at his friend and then dropped his gaze again, ashamed of the foolishness of his own heart, and of the weight of his pride. "I ought to have listened to you from the very beginning. Yes, I am a scoundrel, but I do not wish to be. Not any longer. I should have heeded your warnings from the start. I ought to have realized that the consequences of my actions would come upon me eventually – and now they have done, much to my eternal shame." He took a breath. "Perhaps it is true that I deserve such consequences but, despite that, I seek a way to remove myself from the cords which currently tie themselves around me."

Lord Marchmont's smile slid from his face.

"This is to do with Lord Anderton?"

It was not truly a question, but rather a statement and Phillip found himself nodding, raking his hand through his hair yet again, no doubt sending it in all directions and making him look most unkempt, but he did not much care about his appearance at present.

"I have asked Lady Yardley for help via the voice of Miss Madeley," he told his friend, only daring to glance at him now and again. "I want very much to find a way out of this situation without injuring the young lady in question."

Lord Marchmont's eyes flared.

"A young lady?" he repeated. "I did not think that Lady Allanthorpe would be considered particularly youthful, not since she has already wed and has now been widowed."

That remark had Phillip closing his eyes as he stopped his pacing, his head dropping forward, his eyes refusing to turn towards his friend.

"Yes, you are correct. Lady Allanthorpe is not a young lady in her first Season or the like," he said softly. "But then again, it was not Lady Allanthorpe I took into my arms some three nights ago." At this, Lord Marchmont's eyes opened wide and Phillip let out a rasping breath of both embarrassment and frustration. The gentleman was just as shocked as he had been upon being told the truth. "You were right." he said softly. "As much as I do not want to admit it, everything you said about Lord Anderton has been proven correct. He is *not* the sort of gentleman I ought ever to have taken a wager with. Indeed, he is a cruel fellow and I wish I was not even *acquainted* with him, given that he is a villain and I..."

His head fell forward as he trailed to a stop. After all, what could he throw at Lord Anderton that he himself was not also guilty of? He was a scoundrel, was he not? Yes, he did not cheat, lie, and deceive in the same manner as Lord Anderton, but he took his pleasure where he wanted and cared nothing for the opinions and considerations of others. In that regard, was he not very similar to Lord Anderton?

"I shall say nothing to add any further weight to your already heavy shoulders." Lord Marchmont shook his head. "I only ask you what it is that I can do to be of aid."

"I do not know." Phillip let out a long, slow breath, passing one hand over his forehead and then looking towards Lady Yardley and Miss Madeley. "You may think that it is foolish of me, but I have spoken to Miss Madeley and asked her to speak to Lady Yardley on my behalf. I am not myself acquainted with Lady Yardley, but I know of her reputation."

"An excellent reputation."

Nodding, Phillip resumed his pacing.

"She is a woman of great integrity. I understand that she

writes 'The London Ledger', but yet is very careful about what she places within it. I know that she does not think well of gossip, but I am certain that a good deal must come to her regardless! I am hopeful that, with such a reputation as this, she is then able to be of assistance to me as I face Lord Anderton and what he has done."

His friend nodded slowly, although there was no look of hope lifting his expression. It was as if he were somewhat afraid that there would be no hope for Phillip and the circumstances in which he now found himself and, as Lord Marchmont looked away, a deep darkness seemed to sink into Phillip's soul.

"She approaches."

Lord Marchmont's quiet murmur had Phillip lifting his head and looking directly into the face of Miss Madeley as she came towards him, her friend by her side once more.

There was no smile on her face but, then again, he could not expect there to be, given what she knew of him. She considered him a rogue, and he had been far too inclined to accept that name, though now it no longer held any sort of delight for him. Instead, he was beginning to feel a deep sense of shame and that sensation had him lowering his gaze as she approached.

"Miss Madeley."

Lord Marchmont murmured the same and, as Phillip glanced at her, he saw how she inclined her head towards Lord Marchmont with a small smile on her lips. That smile fell away as she turned her attention towards Phillip, not turning her eyes away as she had done before, but looking directly at him. Phillip's breath caught in his chest, a swirl of nervousness in his stomach as he waited for her to speak. This was the only avenue he had to take, the only path where he thought he might have a little hope. Would it be snatched away from him before he had even begun to walk it?

"Lord Brookmire." Miss Madeley lifted her chin a notch. "Lady Yardley will speak with you."

She said nothing more. There was no smile in her voice, no sympathy lingering in her expression - but what more could he expect? He could not think that he would be offered any genuine concern from her. He had already done so much to cause insult, that it was foolishness to think she might be anything other than cold.

Closing his eyes, he put one hand to his heart.

"Thank you." Lifting his head, he looked directly at her. "Would you be kind enough to make the introductions, then?"

"You ask a great deal of Miss Madeley."

Lord Marchmont lifted an eyebrow and cleared his throat as Miss Madeley shot a glance toward him. Much to Phillip's surprise, she then went on to smile, although it was not at him, but directed to Lord Marchmont instead.

"He does, does he not?" She shook her head, tutting lightly. "I am glad to see that a gentleman such as yourself is aware of it, Lord Marchmont."

Lord Marchmont chuckled.

"Of course. Miss Madeley. I am very much aware of the sort of gentleman that my friend purports to be. I do not doubt that you, as a lady of quality, have silently determined to stay far from his company and that, I concede, would be a very wise decision. The fact that he has now practically compelled you to not only speak to Lady Yardley on his behalf but to now introduce him means, to my mind, that he asks a vast amount from your kindness." He lifted an eyebrow in Phillip's direction and shame immediately pushed itself all the deeper into Phillip's heart. "You have a compassionate heart."

Phillip, listening to the exchange, felt his heart sinking low. It was foolishness to think that there could ever be something of importance between himself and Miss Madeley, especially when he had shown her such disregard in how he had behaved but, yet, there was something about the way she smiled at Lord Marchmont which unsettled him greatly.

"I am grateful to you." He cleared his throat, catching the attention of his friend and Miss Madeley. "Perhaps you might...?"

Turning his gaze towards Lady Yardley, he saw Miss Madeley turn around immediately, leaving Phillip to follow her. The weight of his guilt still sat heavily on his shoulders, and he did not miss the sharp-eyed look Lady Yardley sent to him when he approached. Introductions were made quickly by Miss Madeley, who then turned her head away, seemingly disinterested in what he had to say. Was she to move away from them? Would she turn her attention elsewhere, or was there a chance that she would linger and hear his explanation? Phillip was not certain whether he wished Miss Madeley to hear his account, given the shame of it... but it seemed that he was to have no choice, for Miss Madeley remained by Lady Yardley's side, regardless.

"I hear that you wished to be introduced to me." Lady Yardley lifted an eyebrow "Is there any particular reason for that?"

Phillip immediately nodded.

"I have no right to ask this, I know. However, I come to seek your help." His head dropped forward as he spoke, for he could not seem to look into Lady Yardley's face, and certainly could not bring his attention to Miss Madeley either. "I have been caught in a situation of my own making, a trap I have, to some extent, set for myself. As I have said, I am all too aware of that. I have no right to ask for aid given my reputation, which is something I wholeheartedly accept. Nonetheless, I must beg of you for it, for if there is anything you can do to be of aid to me, it is not only myself you will be of aid to, but also to a young lady of quality."

Lady Yardley lifted an eyebrow, but Miss Madeley merely rolled her eyes, clearly unconvinced. Something like anger threatened to fill Phillip's heart, only for him to then silently shake his head and chase the emotion away. He deserved this. He ought to have expected that she would not believe him, not after how he had behaved - not only towards her, but to so many others.

"Might you explain further?" Lady Yardley spread her hands. "I do not understand fully as yet."

Phillip took a breath.

"Lord Anderton asked if I would take on a wager with him." Knowing that he had to explain it all, he became aware of heat rising up in his face, but continued regardless. "I am ashamed even to repeat what I did, for Lord Marchmont warned me against taking on a wager against Lord Anderton, but I, in my overconfidence and arrogance, did so nonetheless." Lady Yardley merely tilted her head. "There is an honorable widow, Lady Allanthorpe." Hating that he was to discuss this in front of Miss Madeley, Phillip kept his eyes averted. "Anderton wagered that I would be unable to... embrace her."

It was the simplest way he could put it, but all the same, mortification sent a fire burning through him.

"And you accepted this wager, believing you could do so."

Nodding, Phillip swallowed hard as Lady Yardley

shared a glance with Miss Madeley who, as yet, had said nothing.

"I will not go into particular details about exactly what took place, but I believed myself successful. Lord Anderton was nearby to witness it, telling me that he did not trust my word – something which I absolutely understood. But it was only when I went to collect my winnings from him that I realized the situation was not as I had thought it to be."

Miss Madeley now turned her eyes to his.

"Then what happened?"

The fact that she had asked him a question was most surprising indeed but, all the same, Phillip dared not look at her.

"Lord Anderton stated that it was not Lady Allanthorpe I had pulled into my arms, but rather another lady, a young lady of some standing, I might add." He took a breath. "The Marquess of Harrogate's daughter."

The swift intake of breath from both ladies was not entirely expected, but all the same, Phillip felt the weight of their shock settle on him.

"How could such a thing be? And how could Lord Anderton know of it?"

Darkness pinched the edge of Phillip's vision.

"I approached Lady Allanthorpe in the darkness of the gardens after she had been led out by Lord Anderton. I believe now, that, in the midst of the crowd, he deliberately took Lady Gwendoline with him instead of Lady Allanthorpe and I, of course, believed it to be none other than Lady Allanthorpe."

Miss Madeley closed her eyes.

"Good gracious."

"And now I am being blackmailed."

Lady Yardley let out a long, heavy breath as though she

had expected such a thing, and Phillip nodded to confirm that what he had said was what she had heard.

"Then you are being blackmailed by Lord Anderton, after he set up the situation deliberately with that purpose in mind."

Phillip ran one hand over his face, turning away slightly, as though even his body could not bear to face Lady Yardley directly.

"He has played me." Even to his own ears, his voice was throaty and weak, and he gritted his teeth for a moment, frustrated with himself. "He states that unless I do what he wishes, *whenever* he wishes it, he will reveal to the Marquess of Harrogate that I have embraced his daughter in this dark fashion. I will say that the lady in question was very willing indeed to go into my arms, but I certainly would never have taken advantage of her had I known it was the Marquess' daughter."

"Are you quite certain of that?"

There was a sharpness to Miss Madeley's voice and Phillip found himself gazing into flashing blue eyes. Miss Madeley's brows were low, her lips pulled flat, and once more, humiliation crept over him.

"I hardly think we need ask such a question, Miss Madeley."

"It is quite all right." Phillip looked directly at Miss Madeley, silencing Lady Yardley's gentle protest. "You are quite right," he told her. "I stated just now that I would never have considered doing such a thing with a Marquess' daughter, but the truth is I may very well have done so last Season. When I was in London last Season, I did whatever I wished, and without care or consequence. I did as I pleased, and I cared very little for anyone else. I had every intention of doing the same this Season. Lord Marchmont, my dear friend, attempted to warn me of my behavior, telling me of the reputation which I was garnering for myself, but I told him that I did not care." His shoulders sank. "The truth is that it is only because of these circumstances that I have begun to reconsider my behavior and my selfishness. I am ashamed to admit it, but I admit it nonetheless." A hard, self-deprecating laugh broke from him. "It is not as though you are unaware of my reputation and my previous behavior. Thus, as I have said, I am fully aware that I deserve no consideration from anyone. My actions are my own and therefore, the consequences are mine to bear. But were it not for this young lady and for the threat that Lord Anderton holds over her head – a threat she is entirely unaware of – then I would not have sought you out, Lady Yardley." Taking a breath, he returned his attention to the other rather than look at Miss Madeley. "I am deeply concerned and entirely uncertain."

A prolonged silence followed as Lady Yardley looked back at him steadily, clearly considering what he had told her. His lip caught between his teeth, his breath tightening in his chest as he waited for her to make her judgment.

"In truth, Lord Brookmire, while I am sorry to hear of what has taken place, I do not understand what you hope for from me. How can I be of aid to you?"

Lady Yardley's soft voice was a comfort in itself, and Phillip closed his eyes briefly, allowing a small swell of relief to rise in his chest.

"If possible, you can tell me whatever you know of Lord Anderton. I must know what it is that Lord Anderton has to gain from his demands and, if there is anything about him which I will be able to use to my advantage, then I should like to hear it." Speaking more quickly now, his words began to tumble out of him. "I also hoped that you might be able to think of a way to use 'The London Ledger' to stop Lord Anderton from being successful in his demands. Or, when he forces my hand, telling me something which I am to be forced to do for him, for fear that he will reveal my name to the Marquess of Harrogate, then mayhap the Ledger could be used somehow as a warning to the person I am to swindle, or cheat or lie to, or whatever it is that Lord Anderton may wish for me to do."

Miss Madeley put both hands on her hips.

"So Lord Anderton is asking you to behave as a scoundrel might. Something you ought to be able to do without any great difficulty, I think."

The irony in her voice was hard for him to accept, but he nodded, looking down at his hands as they clasped tightly in front of him.

"It is as you say, although I will profess that doing anything which Lord Anderton asks of me would be entirely against my will. I do not want to injure a young lady's reputation beyond saving. I do not want to cause a scandal for a lady of sound reputation simply because Lord Anderton demands it. I do not want to do any of the things which Lord Anderton might ask of me, like taking coin from an already impoverished gentleman or breaking asunder a friendship, simply because Lord Anderton states that I must. Yes, I have brought this upon myself. I have no right to ask for aid but I am doing so in the hope that your hearts are a good deal more compassionate than my own."

"I understand, Lord Brookmire."

Lady Yardley put a hand to his arm for just a moment.

"As do I." Miss Madeley sighed softly and looked away. "After hearing what you have said, I share your concern for those amongst society who might be injured by Lord Anderton and his decrees."

"Indeed. But there is more," Lady Yardley told him softly "I will help you in the hope that you might find yourself to be a better gentleman at the end of this circumstance."

Phillip blinked.

"I do not fully understand."

Lady Yardley smiled a little sadly.

"You state that these consequences are of your own making and, with that statement I quite agree. However, one must hope that in finding out such a thing, you are inclined to change your ways. This is an opportunity for you to make certain that your previous behavior does not continue, an opportunity to reform your character. I am certain that it will be a very difficult transition, for it will take a good deal of consideration of your character which will bring pain to your heart. However, I can assure you that this is for the best. You are a gentleman who could be well thought of, who could be highly regarded rather than pushed away. *That* is why I will aid you, Lord Brookmire. It is not because I think you worthy of such a thing - your behavior has shown you to be quite the opposite! I will, however, do what I can to help you for your own sake *and* to make certain that other members of society, innocent ladies and gentlemen, can be protected from both yourself and Lord Anderton."

Feeling a little like an errant child being chastised by a schoolmistress or strict parent, Phillip bowed his head and fell silent after murmuring only a brief 'thank you'.

"I will aid you too if I can."

Lifting his head in astonishment, Phillip stared at Miss Madeley, only to see her eyes flare with the same surprise. Perhaps she had not expected to say such a thing. Perhaps she had not had any intention of responding in such a manner, but had done so, nonetheless. He offered a small smile, his heart reminding him of just how little he deserved her consideration.

"Thank you, Miss Madeley. You are more generous than I could ever have imagined. Your kind heart and forgiving spirit speak very highly of your character." Taking a breath, he looked to Lady Yardley. "I thank you again, also, Lady Yardley. What is it that I should do first?"

The lady smiled briefly.

"Nothing," she responded as he lifted his eyebrows in surprise. "Lord Anderton will come to you very soon, I am sure, with some sort of demand. That is precisely why he has orchestrated this situation - so that you have no other choice but to do as he requires. When he does make his demand of you, I would ask you to come to speak with me again. Together, we can find a way to make certain that whoever it is he has targeted will remain free of his attack, and that you and Lady Gwendoline, as a result, will be safe also."

Phillip nodded, then tried to speak but found his throat rather tight. Feeling overwhelmed by the kindness of both Lady Yardley and Miss Madeley and utterly ashamed of his own behavior, he inclined his head before turning on his heel and walking quickly away.

CHAPTER SEVEN

"*I*t was somewhat surprising to hear you offer your aid to Lord Brookmire."

Fully aware that this had been a most extraordinary thing to come out of her mouth, Deborah closed her eyes and shook her head, finding no explanation for it.

Lady Yardley smiled.

"Given your expression, I think that you were a little astonished yourself."

Taking a breath, Deborah looked at Lady Yardley and decided to be truthful.

"Yes, I was. I had no intention of saying anything of the sort, and the next thing I knew, I had offered Lord Brookmire my help! I am not the sort of person to take back my word... and now, I confess, I find myself somewhat eager to help him."

A flush of embarrassment crept over her skin, but Lady Yardley's smile only softened.

"It is very kind of you to do so. I will confess that I do not think I have ever seen a gentleman so utterly perplexed and as dismayed as he was during our conversation." Her smile faded. "It is somewhat distressing to see, but as I have said, I am hopeful that this experience will bring about a change in him. I do think Lord Brookmire has every hope of being an excellent gentleman if he just permitted himself to be so."

Her embarrassment over her own honesty still growing, Deborah demanded silently that she continue to speak honestly, for the confusion lingering in her soul these last few days was almost continually in her thoughts, perplexing her gravely. Mayhap sharing it with Lady Yardley would help chase some of that confusion away.

"That may be so, Lady Yardley, and yet my own opinion of Lord Brookmire is still based entirely on what I have heard of him, and from our infrequent interactions." She took a breath. "Which is all the more reason for me to remain entirely disinclined towards him, but yet I..."

Her gaze moved away from Lady Yardley, as she found herself struggling to speak honestly when looking directly at the lady. In the quiet moments that followed, Deborah's thoughts turned again to Lord Brookmire, and she wondered again about her unexpected response to his nearness, recalling the uncertainty which had been in his expression, and the sentiments he had expressed thereafter when speaking with Lady Yardley. It was not as though she liked the gentleman, and certainly not as though she trusted his motivations, but all the same, despite her promise to her mother to avoid him in whatever way she could, she had offered to do the very opposite!

Her lips twisted, remembering how her body had flamed with a sudden and strange heat as he had taken her hand, over and over again, tying their fingers together at the last. How curious it was that she should desire such a thing again, even though she ought to be turning away from him at every opportunity!

"Is there something more to Lord Brookmire's acquaintance with you?"

Lady Yardley interrupted Deborah's thoughts, and she flinched at the sound of Lady Yardley's voice. She had been so lost within herself that she had quite forgotten where she was. Looking at Lady Yardley, Deborah immediately trilled a laugh, but it was much too high-pitched and far too loud to be genuine, and from the smile which spread across Lady Yardley's face, it was clear that she was aware of it.

"Is it that you have an interest in Lord Brookmire? I thought that you disliked him, and I was encouraging you in your avoidance of him."

Deborah closed her eyes.

"I ought to be staying far from him and, until our conversation with him at the ball, I found myself utterly disinclined towards him." Aware that heat was yet again searing through her, she closed her eyes and gave a small, broken laugh. "It is foolishness, is it not?"

"You need not say anything to me that you do not wish to." Lady Yardley smiled gently, her hands clasped lightly in her lap. "I do not judge your feelings, Deborah. In truth, it is not unusual for a young lady to have a somewhat unexpected reaction to a gentleman's nearness. It is all the more confusing if the gentleman is one whom you ought not to even consider!"

"*And* when I am considering Lord Cleverley also!" Deborah flung out both hands and Lady Yardley's eyebrows threw themselves towards her hairline. "Lord Cleverley is an excellent gentleman. He is amiable, good-natured, and well thought of through all of London society. When he asked me to take a walk in the park, I accepted him, and I did enjoy my time with him. Lord Cleverley is a pleasure to talk with, and we seem to share a great many interests. I think him quite delightful and certainly would be glad to be in his company in such a way again, I am sure."

Silence flooded the room again and Deborah went to close her eyes, only to rise from her chair in a sudden pique, her hands clenching and unclenching as she made her way to the window.

"You must find it very disconcerting to be caught up with Lord Brookmire rather than with Lord Cleverley. I can imagine that having very few feelings for Lord Cleverley, a gentleman who is meant to be quite perfect for you and instead catching yourself responding most unexpectedly to Lord Brookmire must leave you somewhat troubled." It was put so well by Lady Yardley that Deborah feared her feelings had been made known to the lady in some way. She turned quickly, only for Lady Yardley to laugh quietly and hold up both hands, her palms out. "No, indeed, my dear. I have no awareness of any specific feelings or emotions on your part. It is only that it is not entirely unexpected for such a thing to take place. Why do you think scoundrels and rogues are so easily able to catch as many ladies as they wish?" She shrugged both shoulders. "It is because of *who* they are and what they do. That is not to say that you are drawn to him because of such a reputation but all the same, gentlemen such as Lord Brookmire are known as rogues and scoundrels because of how quickly and easily they are able to charm the ladies of society. Lord Brookmire is no different, although thus far you have not given in to anything which he has offered you."

Frustrated, Deborah threw up her hands again.

"But I do not want to feel this way." A flood of relief rushed through her as she began to speak of her heart to

Lady Yardley. "When he took my hand, I felt such a heat that I could not find words to respond to what he was saying! It was both extraordinary and deeply concerning to me, for, when out walking with Lord Cleverley, I had placed my arm upon his but..." Her shoulders dropped. "I felt nothing of the same as I felt with Lord Brookmire."

"And you are disappointed with that?"

Lady Yardley waited as Deborah considered her feelings.

"I am not certain whether I feel disappointed or confused by this whole matter." Deborah let her hands rise for a moment, only to then drop them back to her sides. "I have always told myself that I did not necessarily need to fall in love with a gentleman immediately. I would spend time with him, yes, and if my feelings did not begin to grow, then we would simply remain acquaintances. I had been hoping that there would be more than one gentleman interested in my company but, as yet, only Lord Cleverley has shown any genuine interest. I have had other gentlemen call upon me, of course, but none of them have asked to take me to the park or for a ride in their phaeton, as he has."

Much to her surprise, Lady Yardley let out a soft exclamation of surprise.

"Oh, my dear girl, it is early enough in the Season for that! Lord Cleverley has perhaps been a little eager in his attempts to woo you. Yes, he has called upon other young ladies, I am sure, but he has, from what I know, only asked *you* to take a walk with him. However," she continued, her smile now gentling. "If you do not feel anything for him, then that is quite acceptable. You need not demand any feelings from yourself as regards Lord Cleverley."

Closing her eyes, Deborah let out a sigh.

"And what should I do about Lord Brookmire?"

Before Lady Yardley could answer, however, a tap came at the door. Lady Yardley held up one hand to Deborah, asking her to wait for a moment as she called to the butler to enter. Deborah was glad to do so, relieved that none of Lady Yardley's staff would overhear their continued conversation about Lord Brookmire. Servants whispered, and Deborah did not want anyone to know that she had perplexing surges of emotion when it came to Lord Brookmire!

"My lady, Lord Brookmire has come to call upon you. He stated that it was rather urgent."

Butterflies flooded Deborah's stomach as Lady Yardley immediately turned to look at her.

"I can ask him to wait, Miss Madeley." Lady Yardley rose from her chair, coming towards Deborah. "We can finish our conversation and once you have taken your leave, I might then speak to Lord Brookmire alone."

Deborah immediately shook her head, cutting off Lady Yardley's concerns.

"It is quite all right, Lady Yardley. Of course he may join us."

Much to her annoyance, however, her stomach immediately began to swirl with a nervousness which she had not expected. The moment that even Lord Brookmire's *name* was mentioned, it sent such a swell of nervousness through her, it was as though tiny birds were flapping their wings frantically in her stomach. Straightening her shoulders, she chased away those birds with a firm shake of her head before making her way back to her chair, her hands clasped lightly in front of her.

"So long as you are certain."

Lady Yardley nodded to the butler, indicating that Lord Brookmire should be shown in. It only took a few moments, but soon Lord Brookmire walked directly into the room, and thereafter both Lady Yardley and Deborah greeted him with a quick curtsey.

"Miss Madeley." Lord Brookmire inclined his head towards her again, his hands going behind his back. "Forgive me, I did not know that you were with Lady Yardley. I would be more than happy to return at another time so that your visit with her is not interrupted."

Deborah shook her head.

"There is no need to do so, Lord Brookmire." She resumed her seat. "I have already said that I would be glad to aid you, and I suppose that this meeting is rather fortuitous, therefore, rather than being a disruption."

She offered him a slightly wry smile, and in response, Lord Brookmire released such a long breath of relief that Deborah was surprised to hear it. Obviously, something had occurred, and the gentleman was eager to share it with Lady Yardley, seemingly now overwhelmed with relief that he would be able to speak of it immediately, instead of being forced to wait.

"Please do be seated."

Lady Yardley indicated for the gentleman to sit near Deborah, and he did so at once, though he now seemed not to know where to rest his eyes. His gaze landed on everything around the room rather than settling on any one object, or indeed any one person. He would not look directly at Lady Yardley, and now would not even so much as glance at Deborah. The longer they waited, the more awkward the silence became. Deborah shared a look with Lady Yardley, but the lady herself only smiled briefly and then looked again towards Lord Brookmire. Perhaps she was well used to this, or simply a good deal more patient than Deborah! She seemed quite content to wait for Lord Brookmire to speak, for him to gather his thoughts into order so that he might share whatever it was which had taken place.

Deborah, however, was much too impatient indeed, so desperate for Lord Brookmire to speak that she had to curl her hands tight into fists to contain her questions. Lord Brookmire sighed heavily again, ran one hand over his eyes, and then, much to Deborah's relief, began.

"I confess that I feel myself to be a fraud to come and speak to you both in this manner." Lord Brookmire shook his head, letting out his breath through clenched teeth, his eyes still averted. "You both know that I am a gentleman of poor reputation. Last summer I did as I pleased and I had every intention of doing the same this Season. I had been warned by Lord Marchmont about my reputation, but I ignored him, quite determined that I cared nothing for being declared a scoundrel. But now that I find myself having been tricked by someone who bears that claim also, I am faced with dark consequences as a result of my own behavior. I find now, because of that, I must acknowledge my own selfishness in a way that I have not done before. When I consider the wager, and all that Lord Anderton has asked me to do, all I see is my self-interest and pride. It is as though I have been standing before a dark and dusty mirror that has not allowed me to see myself as I truly am. Now, however, the mirror is beginning to become clear and I am not delighted with what I face." Scowling, he dropped his head forward, his voice low. "I have a great deal to consider as regards my own character, and the reputation which I know I hold. I say this not so that you will be impressed with my determination nor in the hope that, by the end of it all, you will think better of me, but simply because I wish to be truthful." His hands fell to either side of the chair. "I *am* a scoundrel. I *am* a rogue and for the first time. I am not certain that I am glad for those words to be associated with me."

Deborah did not know what to say. Certainly, Lord Brookmire appeared to be more than genuine, but surely she knew better than to simply believe him? Her mother's whispers ran through her, reminding her that rogues and scoundrels took what they wanted and said what they pleased, particularly when they wanted to be believed. To her surprise, however, Lady Yardley was the one nodding, as though she already believed Lord Brookmire's words, despite the fact that she herself knew all too well of his reputation.

"You do have a great deal to consider, Lord Brookmire." Lady Yardley's voice was calm and clear. "Unfortunately, that is not something I, nor Miss Madeley, can aid you with. Your reputation - or lack thereof - is entirely your own matter, but if there is something more you would wish to share with us, then please do so now."

At that moment, the tea tray was brought in, and Deborah offered to pour for Lady Yardley. She did so carefully, considering what Lord Brookmire had said, and glancing at him when she set the tea before him. Lord Brookmire himself appeared most distressed, for he was still glancing away from her; his eyes were heavy with shadows and his forehead lined. He only gave her a brief murmur of thanks, as if he were distracted by his thoughts, swamped by all that he thought and felt. For the first time, a measure of sympathy warmed Deborah's heart. She tried to chase it away, but it only grew, demanding that she feel something more for this gentleman.

"Thank you, Deborah." Lady Yardley smiled then looked to Lord Brookmire, lifting an eyebrow as she did so.

"Now, Lord Brookmire. What is it that Lord Anderton has said to you?"

Lord Brookmire's voice remained low.

"Lord Anderton approached me only an hour ago. I was in White's and he appeared by my side, demanding that we speak together. I do not know whether he had been looking for me, or simply happened upon me, but regardless, he has made himself quite clear."

Unable to help herself, Deborah spoke up.

"And what is it that you are to do?"

Finally, Lord Brookmire turned his green eyes to hers, eyes which lacked any sort of sparkle or glint. There were smudges beneath them and his face paled as he began to explain.

"I am to steal away Lady Jemima from the gentleman who is courting her at present."

His jaw tightened as he dropped his gaze to the floor.

"But – but why?"

The horror which filled Deborah's voice must have made its way to Lord Brookmire's ears, given how badly he winced.

"I do not think that Lord Anderton has any reason other than the sheer dark delight, of damaging other people's lives."

"Does he know either party well?" Lady Yardley asked, but Lord Brookmire shook his head.

"Lord Anderton certainly has no desire to marry, so he does not intend to take Lady Jemima for himself, but yet my instructions are quite clear."

"Goodness."

Her voice was a whisper as something heavy dropped into the pit of Deborah's stomach.

"I have heard that Lady Jemima is being courted by

THE VISCOUNT'S UNLIKELY ALLY | 89

Lord Williamston." Lady Yardley tilted her head a little. "I wonder if Lord Anderton has something against the gentleman."

"He does appear to be a gentleman who holds a grudge." Lord Brookmire spread his hands wide for a moment. "I could see him doing such a thing. It may be a good thought, Lady Yardley."

"If he has something against the gentleman then, while he seeks to break apart Lord Williamston and Lady Jemima, he will be able to do so from a distance. That means that he has no responsibility whatsoever."

Lady Yardley murmured her comment as Lord Brookmire gazed at her.

"Yes, that would make sense." Lord Brookmire squeezed his eyes closed. "I confess that, had I noticed Lady Jemima myself at the start of the Season, I would have cared very little as to whether or not she was already being courted. However, with Lord Anderton asking this of me, I can see the darkness of it. I become more and more ashamed, the more I realize about myself."

Again surprised by Lord Brookmire speaking with such apparent honesty, Deborah looked away sharply at the realization that she was beginning to believe him.

"Lady Jemima is not yet betrothed to Lord Williamston, however." Lady Yardley mused, tapping one finger on her chin. "They have been courting since the beginning of the Season, however."

Lord Brookmire nodded.

"Yes, I believe that is so. I was in conversation with Lady Essington, her mother, at the very beginning of this foolishness. She was attempting to not only keep her daughter from becoming distracted by other gentlemen, but also to keep Lord Williamston's attention fixed on Lady

Jemima. I do not know precisely why, but I suspect that mayhap both Lady Jemima and Lord Williamston might be inclined towards easy distraction."

A sudden thought came to Deborah's mind, and she chuckled, bringing two wide-eyed looks of astonishment to her. Heat ran through her cheeks as she attempted to explain her response, a little embarrassed at having to do so.

"Forgive me. It was only that I thought it sounded as though both Lady Jemima and Lord Williamston are equal in kind when it comes to their nature." she finished, shrugging lightly as she spoke. "Perhaps it would be best for them both if they *were* to be betrothed."

It was something of an idle thought, and she was about to say that, only for Lord Brookmire to suddenly slap his knee and exclaim aloud, making Deborah jump in surprise.

"That is it then, surely?" His eyes suddenly sparkled, a smile flooding his features with new-found excitement. "They must become betrothed! A betrothal is very different from courtship, surely? It holds a good deal more weight." A small chuckle escaped from him as he rose from his chair, suddenly striding around the room, his arms flinging up wildly. "The Marquess of Essington is not a gentleman to be feared, but to be highly respected. I do not think that Lord Anderton would instruct me to break the betrothal between Lady Jemima and Lord Williamston. He would not dare to do so, I am sure of it."

Lady Yardley tilted her head.

"How can you be so certain of it?" she asked softly "Lord Anderton might very well state that you ought to do so, for you must recall that he is the one who will not be blamed for it in any way. Only you will carry the guilt."

Deborah watched as Lord Brookmire's shoulders

slumped, only for him to suddenly spring to life again, his eyes blazing with hope now.

"Yes, but should such a thing happen, then I would be quite ruined. I might break the betrothal, but to do such a thing as that would make certain that I would be driven from London. I would be given the cut direct by so many people, I would never be able to show my face in London again. Lord Anderton would lose his advantage, would he not?" He slammed one fist into the palm of the other hand. "Yes, I am quite determined. I think this must be the only way forward. Thank you, Miss Madeley, for that suggestion." His exuberance was somewhat overwhelming, and Deborah could nod before he then looked Lady Yardley. "Do you think, Lady Yardley, that it can be done?" Coming to sit back in his seat, Lord Brookmire perched on the edge of it and leaned forward. "Do you think you might be able to use the Ledger to encourage a betrothal between Lord Williamston and Lady Jemima?"

Deborah licked her lips, seeing Lady Yardley frown. There was no reason for her to do such a thing, other than to protect Lady Jemima from the machinations of Lord Anderton. But would that in itself be enough of a reason?

"I am sure that I can think of something to write."

Lady Yardley smiled, and immediately Lord Brookmire's head dropped forward, a rush of breath escaping from him. A small smile crossed Deborah's lips, but she quickly fought to hide it before he looked at her. Losing her fight, she looked into Lord Brookmire's eyes as he lifted his head, the smile still on her lips, only for him to shake his head again.

"I am profoundly in your debt." He looked at Deborah for a long moment, and instantly, a warmth began to curl through her. She tried to tug her gaze away, but it seemed to him to be stuck steadfastly to him. It was only when Lady Yardley clapped her hands in evident relief that the moment shattered.

"This is very good." Sounding pleased, Lady Yardley smiled towards Deborah, who nodded and then picked up her tea so that she could take a sip of it, rather than becoming distracted by Lord Brookmire's presence again. "I confess, Lord Brookmire, that I have been a little reluctant to aid you, but in this matter, I am relieved that you came to speak to me," Lady Yardley continued. "Both Lady Gwendoline and Lady Jemima should not be put in harm's way by anyone, particularly not by a gentleman whose maneuverings are simply for his own ends."

Lord Brookmire nodded eagerly.

"Yes, it is precisely as you say, Lady Yardley. Again, pray do not think that I am unaware of how little I deserve this." Rising from his chair, he bowed to them both. "I look forward to seeing what it is that you can place in the Ledger, Lady Yardley, and thank you again, Miss Madeley, for your wonderful suggestion. I do not think that we would have come upon the idea, had you not said anything."

Deborah too inclined her head, aware that the heat which he set in her by simply a single look still lingered.

"But of course, Lord Brookmire. I do hope that Lady Jemima and Lord Williamston soon find themselves very happy."

Lord Brookmire smiled a little ruefully, then turned to the door.

"As do I, Miss Madeley. As do I."

CHAPTER EIGHT

"*W*ell?" Lord Anderton narrowed his gaze at Phillip. "Do you have any intention of approaching her this evening? I want this done quickly, if you recall."

It was most unfortunate that Phillip had attended the same soiree as Lord Anderton, but his presence had not been entirely unexpected. Given that both gentlemen were equals in society, it was to be expected that they would be invited to the same functions. It had only been a day since he had spoken to Lady Yardley and as yet, he had heard nothing from either herself or Miss Madeley.

"I have been considering your request." Knowing that Lord Anderton was waiting for an answer, Phillip kept his chin lifted, refusing to flinch as Lord Anderton chuckled darkly. "It is not particularly fair on the young Lady Jemima, I must say. I find that particularly abhorrent."

"You do not mean to say that you are averse to it?"

The irony in Lord Anderton's voice was not hidden from Phillip but, as he grinned, the shadow hidden behind it sent a shudder running through Phillip's frame.

"I would state that I am *very* much averse to it." Phillip folded his arms across his chest. "It is unfair to the young lady."

"And yet you would have said very little about such a thing had this not been forced upon you, I am sure!" Getting to the heart of the matter, Lord Anderton laughed again, and Phillip looked away. "You know very well that you would previously have cared very little as to whether or not the young lady was being courted by another gentleman. If you saw a pretty young lady you wished to embrace, then you would have done so as soon as you could, and without even a second thought."

"That may very well be true, but that is not my perspective now." One shoulder lifted. "I am, mayhap, becoming a little less of a scoundrel. I intend to reform myself."

This statement brought nothing but laughter, and Phillip simply had to stand and endure it, for he could not simply leave the conversation for fear that Lord Anderton would follow him and, thereafter, their ongoing conversation would be overheard by someone else.

"Do not think that you have any power here now, nor that I will believe your words about reforming yourself." Lord Anderton waved one hand, as if dismissing Phillip entirely. "You are nothing but a scoundrel, and you shall always be a scoundrel. Regardless of your promises and intentions, you will do as I have asked." He grinned broadly. "I do not think that I need to remind you about the consequences of refusing me."

Phillip's jaw jutted forward, his hands clenching into fists as rage began to boil through him.

"Why do you do this?"

"It is not your business."

"You do not like Lord Williamston, is that not so? *That*

is why you are intent on chasing away his young lady. You wish to injure him for some slight he did you, which is why you now seek to separate them."

Lord Anderton scowled - the first time he had not laughed since Phillip and he had begun their conversation.

"My reasons do not matter. At least they do not matter to you." His smile returned quickly. "All that concerns you is that you remove Lady Jemima from Lord Williamston. Are you going to do that or not?"

Everything in Phillip wanted to state that he would do nothing of the sort, only to remember that he had no other course but to agree. To refuse would put him in danger immediately, and would also cause great suffering to Lady Gwendoline – someone he had already injured by embracing her without warning.

"If I must." Gritting his teeth hard to contain his fury, he took a deep breath. "But you should not think that my actions will be hasty. Such things will take time, as I am sure you are aware."

Lord Anderton shook his head.

"No, you will not take a great deal of time. You will do this as quickly as you possibly can, just as you would have done the previous Season... before you decided that you had a conscience." An ugly expression wrapped across his face, his eyes growing a little hooded, his lip curling into a snarl. "I have no time for you to wait or to linger in the hope that I will change my mind. You shall do as you are asked, and you shall do so immediately. I want it done by this week's end."

So saying, he turned sharply with his back to Phillip and strode away. Phillip closed his eyes, waiting for his ire to ebb just a little, so that he did not go after Lord Anderton, grab him by the lapels, and hiss that he would do nothing of the sort. After some moments, he was finally able to breathe a little more easily and, clasping his hands behind his back, he chose to wander around the room. Many gentlemen nodded to him, and certainly there were a good many ladies who caught his eye, but Phillip did not linger. Instead, his mind remained fixed on the situation with Lord Anderton, silently praying that Lady Yardley had taken on Miss Madeley's suggestion, as she had said she would do, and that soon, this dark weight would be tugged free of his shoulders. His lips lifted briefly as he thought of Miss Madeley. Her idle remark had been the only thing that had brought light to his mind and, had she remained silent, then his situation might have been very dark indeed.

As he continued to meander around the shadows at the edges of the room, a sudden exclamation caught his attention. He lifted his head, seeing a gentleman being clapped on the back by one or two others and, confused, Phillip made his way towards them. Someone laughed and another made a remark which had one particular gentleman's face flush red – a gentleman Phillip recognized.

Lord Williamston.

"Whatever is this I have come upon?"

Keeping his tone light, he looked around the small group, his eyes going to Lord Williamston at the last. As he watched, Lord Williamston's face flushed scarlet and he rubbed one hand over the back of his neck.

"There is nothing the matter." Lord Williamston shrugged and rolled his eyes. "It is only that something has been suggested, and given that I have not refuted it, I confess now that my intentions have become clear, albeit before I have spoken to the lady!"

Phillip looked from one grinning face to the next, not quite grasping what was being said.

"He does not understand." Lord Greenwood nudged

Phillip lightly. "You have not read 'The London Ledger' then? It was only handed out this afternoon, so I suppose that cannot be held against you!"

A flurry of hope sent sparks through Phillip's heart. He looked back at Lord Williamston, who was by now, grinning broadly.

"I had heard that there was a certain attachment to a particular lady," he remarked, with a slow smile beginning to spread across his face - a genuine one that spoke of both relief and happiness. "I was in conversation with Lady Essington only a few days ago and she stated that there was a connection between yourself and her daughter. Is it to this that these gentlemen are referring?"

Lord Williamston chuckled.

"Yes, it is so. There is a note in 'The London Ledger' that there will soon be a betrothal announced and the initials of those mentioned speak only of myself and Lady Jemima. I am not in the least bit upset, however, for I will not pretend that my desire has not been for such a thing for some time. Therefore, I will do nothing to refute it."

Delighted with this, Phillip stuck out one hand and shook Lord Williamston's firmly.

"I assume that you are to propose to Lady Jemima?"

The man nodded.

"Just as soon as I am able. I have already gained Lord Essington's blessing, albeit some time ago. I have been tardy in asking her, finding myself struggling with finding the right moment and the correct words – but that shall not be the case any longer. I hope that, by the end of this evening, you shall all find me a betrothed gentleman."

Phillip's heart lifted at the cheers and laughter which went up at this statement.

"In truth, I am very glad for you, Lord Williamston. I do

hope that you and Lady Jemima find happiness together. I am sure that she is an excellent creature."

"And brings a large dowry with her," cried another gentleman, making the entire group laugh.

"And to be acquainted with a Marquess in such a close connection can do no harm to your standing," chimed in another.

The group rattled with laughter, and Phillip took a small step back, so overwhelmed with relief, he could barely speak. It seemed that Lady Yardley *had* placed something within 'The London Ledger' and, happily, Lord Williamston had responded with delight and clear anticipation to the idea of proposing to Lady Jemima. It also now meant that there was nothing to be gained from Lord Anderton attempting to break up the connection between gentleman and lady, save for having Phillip pushed from society should he attempt to do so... and then be discovered. He now had to hope that Lord Anderton would back away from this particular idea.

"I thought you might wish to see 'The London Ledger', Lord Brookmire."

A soft voice reached his ears, and Phillip turned quickly, only to look directly into the eyes of Miss Madeley. She was smiling warmly, and Phillip took a deep breath before taking the paper from her, aware that his heart had quickened simply from looking into her face.

"Miss Madeley." He did not glance at the paper but held his gaze to hers. "Your wonderful suggestion seems to have brought about great satisfaction. Lord Williamston is to propose to Lady Jemima and therefore, I hope, it will bring an end to the matter with Lord Anderton, for the moment at least." He inclined his head. "I am in your debt."

Miss Madeley's smile faded just a little.

"I do not want Lady Jemima to be at all injured." She lifted her shoulders gently. "But in addition, if it is as you say, then I am glad for you also, for if you are true in your desire to become a repentant fellow, then I think that would be for the best – not only for you, but for all of society." A wry smile tilted the corner of her mouth as she tipped her head gently. "After all, it would be to every young lady's advantage if you were not to be a cruel fellow who did not care anything for the feelings of others."

Phillip shook his head.

"I can assure you, my intentions are entirely true. True change will, I admit, take me some time, but my path towards redemption is already laid out for me, I am sure." He looked at her for a long moment, his heart suddenly turning over on itself as though it were delighting in the company of Miss Madeley. A little embarrassed by what he felt, he quickly turned his attention to 'The London Ledger', looking down to see the paper filled with various stories of interest. A gentle hand pointed to where the news came of Lord Williamston, and Phillip read it quickly.

"'It has been said that one Lord W. has spoken to the Marquess of Essington as regards the company of his daughter. It is hoped and expected by all those who care for both, that a betrothal will soon take place.'"

Phillip looked up quickly.

"That is precisely what Lord Williamston said to me only a moment ago. He stated that he had spoken with Lord Essington some time ago, but had thereafter been somewhat tardy as he sought to find the right moment to propose to Lady Jemima."

Miss Madeley smiled, and this time, her eyes lit.

"I believe that we have Lady Yardley and her connections to thank for that bit of information." Laughing softly, she lifted a shoulder. "It seems that Lady Yardley knows a great deal, but says very little. I am only glad that Lord Williamston took this so well." Her gaze slid towards the fellow where he stood behind Phillip. "At least, he appears to be rather pleased."

Phillip chuckled.

"He certainly is. I see it is certainly a wise decision – at least, for Lord Williamston. He will be settled with one young lady, and that will be the end of things. I do hope that they will be very contented."

"Do you truly believe that contentedness can come from being suitably and happily married, or do you say such things only to placate me?" Miss Madeley lifted her eyebrows in question. "I would have thought a gentleman with your reputation would scorn such things."

"And you would have been quite correct." Phillip now dropped his head so that he would not have to look at her, finding that his shame was quick to mount whenever she studied him with that arched eyebrow and a question in her eyes – a question which, in this case, she clearly already knew the answer to. "You torment me, Miss Madeley." With a sigh, he licked his lips "Yes, I confess it. I would not have thought matrimony an excellent situation, had you asked me earlier this Season. In fact, I would have laughed at it, telling you that a gentleman did not need to marry until it was absolutely required; that they were, in fact, throwing their future away, tossing aside a great deal of potential happiness. I would have believed that they could have enjoyed the Season for many a year before taking a wife and said that they were all foolish to do so before it was necessary." There was no reason for him not to speak honestly, given that she already knew the answer to what she had asked and thus, he did not hold himself back. "Lady

THE VISCOUNT'S UNLIKELY ALLY | 101

Yardley states that I will have a great deal of time to think upon my own character, and she is right in that. I am relieved that Lord Williamston and Lady Jemima will be betrothed, for it will free them from Lord Anderton's attack but..." Looking over his shoulder, he paused for a moment. "Now I see the smile on Lord Williamston's face and the happiness in his eyes and I believe it is genuine. I confess that I have not thought about such a thing before, I have not imagined that happiness could be gained from being so devoted to only one other."

Clearing his throat and feeling a little abashed, he handed back the Ledger to Miss Madeley, and their fingers brushed as he did so. A jolt ran through him, and his breath hitched in his chest, forcing him to suck in air. Their eyes met and caught, holding together for a long moment, a moment which seemed to grow into the longest time, and yet could not have been more than a few seconds. The sound of this soiree faded until the only sound in his ears was his roaring heartbeat. Miss Madeley did not look away from him, nor did he pull his eyes from her. Whatever was it that he was feeling, and... could she see it in his face? Why was it that she who had perplexed him from their first meeting now perplexed him in an entirely different way?

"Miss Madeley, Lord Brookmire."

Lady Yardley came to smile at them, and Phillip immediately inclined his head, breaking his connection with Miss Madeley, and finding himself somewhat relieved that he had done so. These strange feelings were something he ought not to be thinking about at the present moment, given that his only consideration was to be Lord Anderton. That was enough trouble for the present.

"Miss Madeley was showing me 'The London Ledger. Thank you, Lady Yardley, for what you have done." Phillip lifted his head and smiled warmly. "It seems as though you have succeeded."

"Only thanks to Miss Madeley." Lady Yardley offered a quick smile to her young friend. "And also thanks to Lady Essington, who was more than happy to tell me of Lord Williamston's visit to Lord Essington at the very start of the Season! It seems that Lady Jemima and Lord Williamston were known to each other last Season, and an interest was certainly there, but nothing certain had taken place. All that was required was a little nudge, for now Lord Williamston is determined to marry Lady Jemima as soon as he can." Her smile was warm, her expression soft. "I am glad for them both."

"As am I." Phillip put one hand to his heart and inclined his head again. "And I am truly grateful to you both."

"Lord Brookmire."

Lord Anderton's booming voice caught Phillip's attention, and he turned his head sharply, only to see the gentleman jerking his head towards the wall behind him, making it quite clear that Phillip was expected to join him immediately.

"Is that Lord Anderton?"

With a small smile of regret, Phillip nodded and excused himself, catching the glance shared between Lady Yardley and Miss Madeley. Wondering what it was that Lord Anderton would say, Phillip made his way across the room and directly towards Lord Anderton, noting that his face had gone very red indeed.

"Did you want something more from me?" Phillip lifted an eyebrow. "I cannot exactly go to speak to Lady Jemima if you are determined to keep calling me over to speak with you."

Folding his arms over his chest, he sighed loudly, but Lord Anderton only sneered.

"As though you had any intention of making your way directly to her." Keeping his voice low, Lord Anderton poked one finger hard into Phillip's chest. "I have seen you speaking only to Lord Williamston with some of the other gentlemen and, thereafter, with Lady Yardley and some other young lady with her. You have not yet even *thought* to go and speak to Lady Jemima! However..." His lips flattened. "This may be in my favor."

Phillip did not allow his lips to even twitch into a smile though inwardly, he prayed that it was as it seemed. Aware that he had to give the appearance of being entirely uncertain about what was taking place, he forced a frown in place of a smile, looking at Lord Anderton steadily.

"What is it that you are speaking of?"

"I have just heard news that Lord Williamston and Lady Jemima are to become betrothed this very evening." Lord Anderton waved his hand and snorted derisively. "Of course, I think it a ridiculous notion, and it is most unfortunate that the gentleman intends to do this but, nonetheless, I cannot break apart a Marquess' daughter and her betrothal. To break apart a courtship would be one thing, but to break a betrothal would be quite another. I may be a rogue, but I am certainly not foolish with it. I know the vehemence which might follow should you do such a thing and then, I would lose my advantage."

Shrugging, Phillip attempted to appear as nonchalant as he could, whilst inwardly rejoicing that Miss Madeley's plan had worked.

"Very well." His hands fell to his sides. "Well, if that is all you wished to say, then I shall make my way back to enjoying the rest of this soiree."

He turned, only for Lord Anderton's hand to shoot out and grab his shoulder.

"Do not think that you have escaped." His voice was low, and Phillip turned around to face him again, stepping back so that the gentleman's hand had to fall from his shoulder. "Do not think that you will get to escape from my intentions. My threat still stands. Regardless of what it is I tell you to do, you shall do it without complaint."

The bubbling anger returned but, controlling it, Phillip again shrugged and turned away. Taking slow breaths, he made his way directly across the room, and as far from Lord Anderton as he could go. Slowly, his furious heartbeat began to slow and then, glancing across the room, he caught Miss Madeley's eye. She had been watching him and, with a sudden thrill, he offered her a smile and received a brilliant one in return. Warmth ran through his entire frame, filling his heart, filling his mind, and giving him the sense of standing a little taller. Thus far, Lord Anderton had been foiled, and while it would not be too long before the next request came, Phillip could only exult that his dark plans had been ruined... and he had Miss Madeley and Lady Yardley to thank for it.

CHAPTER NINE

"*W*hat say you to a ride in my phaeton? I do recall suggesting that to you, Miss Madeley, during some prior conversation but, as yet, we have not arranged it."

Lord Cleverley smiled warmly at Deborah, but she did not smile in response. Even when in conversation with Lord Cleverley, her thoughts had been almost entirely upon Lord Brookmire, and whether or not Lord Anderton had made yet another demand upon him during these last few days. Nothing had been said between them since the soiree, and with every day that passed with no news coming, she was beginning to find her every moment filled with thoughts of Lord Brookmire. It was utterly disconcerting and even now, while she was in the midst of the fashionable hour in Hyde Park and meant to be speaking with Lord Cleverley, she struggled to pull her thoughts away from the gentleman.

"That is very kind of Lord Cleverley, is it not?"

Lady Prescott nudged Deborah gently, and she quickly forced a smile, having lost what Lord Cleverley was saying, given how clouded her thoughts had become.

"Yes, that is very generous of you, Lord Cleverley." Making to smile, she tilted her head. "Of course, I should have to speak with my father before I could agree to such a thing, since I will not be able to take a maid or companion with me."

Quickly, she glanced at her mother, who had opened her mouth, no doubt to say that she was sure Lord Prescott would be amenable, only for her mouth to snap shut as Deborah gave a minute shake of her head; an action which, thankfully, Lord Cleverley did not catch.

"Then perhaps I shall come to take tea and ask him myself... and mayhap not only about the ride in the phaeton."

Lord Cleverley's broad smile sent light into his eyes, but again, Deborah did not join him in his delight. Instead, her stomach twisted sharply as she looked quickly to Lord Cleverley, wondering what he meant by such a thing. To ask a lady's father about certainty over a phaeton ride was a little overzealous. Surely could not be that he thought to ask for courtship. He had only come to take tea twice with her and they had walked it in the park only once. To be thinking of anything more would be, to her mind, a little presumptuous.

"You are very kind." Deborah cleared her throat gently, choosing to be honest as she always had been before. "As you know, I have had other gentlemen calling upon me also, Lord Cleverley. For myself, it is rather early in the Season to be thinking about anything of a particularly serious nature. After all," she continued, putting a smile on her face. "I am sure that I am not the only young lady you have sat down to take tea with."

Lord Cleverley's eyes flew wide, only for him to then chuckle and nod in her direction, though her face was a little flushed now.

"You may be quite correct there, Miss Madeley." He gave a slight lift of his shoulders. "And while I will not deny taking tea with numerous other young ladies, I have not asked any of them to join me for a walk in the park, save for you."

Her stomach twisted again as Deborah struggled to know how to respond. She did not want to give Lord. Cleverley an impression of happiness over this remark, but nor did she want him to think that she disliked his company. However, she was certainly not ready for him to even *contemplate* courtship with her as yet, particularly when her thoughts were weighted towards an entirely different gentleman altogether!

And when I feel more for him than I do for Lord Cleverley.

This strange consideration sent tremors through her, and she shivered lightly, only for Lord Cleverley to exclaim that she must be cold, thinking that the sun was little too low in the sky for the ladies of the *ton*. Deborah, however, only laughed.

"Good gracious, Lord Cleverley. I am not as delicate as all that." With a smile, she tilted her head. "It is not cold, not by any means. However, I do appreciate your consideration and concern for me."

Thankfully, at this juncture, Lord Cleverley seemed quite contented to leave her be and excused himself, stating that he had seen an acquaintance he wished very much to speak to. With a slow breath of relief escaping her, Deborah watched him depart, only to turn her head and gaze into the sharp eyes of her mother.

"You did not give Lord Cleverley a particularly eager response." Her head tilted. "Is there a reason for that?"

Deborah, seeing the flash in her mother's eyes, winced.

"Would you be greatly displeased with me if I were not to give him a great deal of encouragement?"

She waited for her mother's response, relieved when Lady Prescott shrugged.

"I would not be overly upset, nor would your father be," came the reply. "However, there must be some reason for it. Why is it that you are drawn away from Lord Cleverley? Do you not think him a kind gentleman?"

"Yes, he is very kind." Deborah glanced over to Lord Cleverley who was now talking with another gentleman. "I am all too aware that he is more than suitable for me as regards a good match but...." Sighing, she spread her hands. "I cannot truly explain it other than to say that there is no intensity of feeling, as I had hoped and expected."

Lady Prescott nodded.

"I see."

"You are not angry with me, I hope?"

"Oh, my dear, of course I am not!" She smiled quickly. "I quite understand that you wish to seek out a gentleman who cares for you, and to whom your heart is also inclined. That is almost admirable, but you may find yourself struggling there. It takes a particular sort of gentleman to fall in love with and who, also, is open to the idea of love."

Instantly, Lord Brookmire flew into her mind and Deborah closed her eyes, as if, in doing so, she could chase away the vision of him. She had no desire to think of him in any such affectionate terms, so why then had he flung himself into her thoughts when her mother had spoken of love?

"Are you quite well, my dear?"

"Yes, Mama." Frustrated, she opened her eyes and looked away from Lady Prescott, silently thinking to herself that it would probably be for the best to inform her mother of Lord Brookmire's presence with Lady Yardley of late. Firstly, she did not want to keep secrets from her mother and secondly, she had no intention of telling her the entirety of the truth. "There is, in fact, something I need to speak with you about." Pausing, she glanced at her mother. Lady Prescott was waiting patiently for her daughter to speak, but by the slight glint in her eyes, Deborah knew that she was already a little concerned.

"It is about Lord Brookmire." Trying to speak as factually as possible, Deborah spread her hands. "He came to call on Lady Yardley while I was visiting her. He did offer to come back at another time, but I did not want him to do so."

Lady Prescott's eyebrows lifted high.

"Lady Yardley spoke with Lord Brookmire?"

Deborah nodded.

"I understand that this may come as a surprise, Mama, for it was to me, but it appears that Lord Brookmire is eager to reform himself. He no longer wishes to be a scoundrel or to hold the reputation of a rogue. Lady Yardley knows a great deal about him and has warned society of his return using 'The London Ledger' but now accepts his willingness to change."

She said no more than this, giving no real reason nor explanation for Lord Brookmire's sudden change of heart. It was with obvious surprise that Lady Prescott's eyes widened.

"You mean to say that Lady Yardley believes him, then?"

Again, Deborah nodded but caught the edge of her lip in her teeth, wondering what her mother would make of all of this.

"It is most extraordinary." Lady Prescott shook her head in disbelief, looking away from Deborah for a moment. "I suppose, with it being Lady Yardley, I would trust her judgment. That being said, however..." Her gaze swooped towards Deborah again. "This does not mean that I want to see you in prolonged conversation with him. It is just as it has been before."

Deborah made to nod, only to hesitate.

"But Mama, if he is truly to reform himself, then how is anyone in society to accept him unless there are those of us willing to greet him, to stand with him, and to converse with him?" She looked away quickly as her mother's eyebrows lifted again. "As long as it is always in company, would it not be all right to have the occasional conversation with him? After all, you have said that you trust Lady Yardley's judgment."

Something flickered in her mother's eyes, and Deborah flushed yet held her gaze steadily. Recalling what both her mother and Lady Yardley had said about gentleman such as Lord Brookmire – the fact that rogues, scoundrels, and rascals were usually able to steal the attention of any lady they sought, given their charm – she began to wonder if that fear was now present in her mother's mind.

"You do have a compassionate heart, Deborah, my dear." Her mother sighed heavily, her lips twisting to one side, perhaps uncertain of whether or not she would agree to this request. After a few more moments, she let out another long breath. "You know that I have encouraged you to think deeply about matters, and to make decisions carefully. Thus far, you have proven that any decision you have made has always been well thought out. You have a generous spirit - however, and I am concerned that Lord

THE VISCOUNT'S UNLIKELY ALLY | 111

Brookmire might take advantage of that. I should not like to see you injured."

"I understand your concerns." Deborah spoke softly as her mother's lips twisted to one side a little. "But you need not worry. I am more than able to be cautious and, at the same time, still a little more open when it comes to Lord Brookmire. As I have said, I was not immediately eager to believe his words, but Lady Yardley's consideration of him has helped me to see the matter in a different light."

"I can understand that." Lady Prescott lifted her hands, then let them fall again. "Do please be cautious, Deborah."

A small flicker of hope lit a candle in Deborah's soul.

"You mean that you will permit me?"

Lady Prescott nodded.

"You were honest enough to speak to me about him and I appreciate your willingness to do so. It means that you are not skulking away in some corner to attempt to spend a little time with him, as so many other young ladies have done!" Laughing rather ruefully, she smiled. "I have heard that the Marquess of Harrogate's daughter is one so inclined. I believe he is having the most terrible time with her."

In an instant, all thoughts of Lord Brookmire flew from Deborah's mind.

"Goodness! Do you mean to say she is...."

"She is a little insensible when it comes to the gentlemen of society." Lady Prescott sighed heavily but looked directly into Deborah's face. "I am grateful to you for being so level-headed. You cannot know the relief it is to be able to trust one's daughter."

Deborah blinked rapidly, barely hearing her mother's compliment, and realizing now that Lord Anderton had taken advantage of Lady Gwendoline's willingness, and, from the sounds of it, somewhat gullible nature. He had led her out of the ballroom, knowing that she would go willingly into Lord Brookmire's arms. Lord Anderton truly was the very worst sort of fellow and, as she considered that fact, her sympathy for Lord Brookmire rose.

Although these consequences were brought upon him by his own actions, said a silent voice in her heart. *But if it is to reform him, then I am almost glad of it.*

At that very moment, she spied none other than Lord Anderton drawing near. Their eyes met for a moment and Deborah's stomach tightened, her back straightening instinctively.

"Might I suggest that you do not particularly like the gentleman who is approaching?"

Her mother's sharp eyes had caught Deborah's change in expression and, glancing back at Lord Anderton and then again to her mother, she shook her head lightly.

"I do not think highly of him, no. I know that he professes to be a gentleman but, by all accounts I have heard, he does not behave so. I do not think him a gentleman to be trusted."

Her mother nodded in evident understanding.

"Then permit me to engage him in conversation while you go and find another one of your friends to speak with." Her eyes flew over Deborah's shoulder. "Look there are Miss Millington and Lady Sherbourne walking together, why do you not join them for a short while? Do stay in sight of me, though, if you please."

With a smile of gratitude, Deborah wasted no time, turning on her heel and hurrying towards her two friends. Miss Millington and Lady Sherbourne were delighted to see her and, after a moment of greeting each other, Deborah looped her arm through Miss Millington's and, together, the three walked away, leaving Lord Anderton and Lady Prescott behind.

~

"Good afternoon."

It was with a slightly horrified look that Miss Millington exchanged a glance with Deborah before inclining her head. Deborah, on the other hand, found herself smiling - first at her friend and then at Lord Brookmire.

"Lord Brookmire. Good afternoon." She bobbed a curtsey, and her heart leaped as he returned her smile. She could only pray that Miss Millington did not notice her flushed cheeks. Lady Sherbourne had escaped to speak to another one of their acquaintances, leaving Deborah and Miss Millington alone together. They were still in view of her mother, of course, and now she had her approval to speak with Lord Brookmire, Deborah did so with an ease of heart and of conscience. "You are acquainted with Miss Millington, I think?"

Lord Brookmire nodded, but there was something in his expression that caught Deborah's attention. This time, his smile did not spread as widely as it usually did, and his green eyes held no brightness.

"Yes, I am."

Again, he bowed, only to shift from one foot to the other, his eyes darting over her shoulder to where Lord Anderton still spoke to Deborah's mother. Was he concerned that Lord Anderton would come to speak with him? Or was it that Lord Anderton had been in conversation with him already?

"And have you had a pleasant afternoon, Lord Brookmire?"

Aware that they could not speak freely at present, Deborah kept her question short and rather direct. Lord Brookmire nodded and smiled again, but it faded quickly.

"Yes, I have. Save for a conversation with a particular gentleman, I have found myself to be quite contented."

Deborah bit her lip, glancing at Miss Millington, who appeared to have very little desire to speak, given that she was staring at the ground. She had no doubt that Lord Brookmire spoke of Lord Anderton, but there was no easy way to ask him what had taken place. Setting her shoulders, she offered him another small smile.

"I am afraid that Lady Yardley is not here with me, although I am to see her this evening." Casting another quick look at her friend, she returned her gaze to Lord Brookmire. "I might, however, be willing to spend a few minutes looking for her, should you wish it. So long as we stay within sight of my mother, I am certain that she would not mind."

A swift intake of breath caught her attention and Deborah kept her smile pinned in place, practically feeling the heat coming from Miss Millington's furious look. With a slight shrug, Deborah smiled again at Lord Brookmire, who immediately offered his arm, his shoulders dropping in evident relief.

"I would be very grateful. I have a great desire to speak with Lady Yardley."

Deborah smiled, understanding fully.

"Of course. Miss Millington, would you wish to join us?"

Miss Millington shook her head.

"I am afraid that I must return to my own mother," she

said rather sharply. "Are you quite certain that *you* do not wish to return to Lady Prescott?"

"Quite certain." Deborah offered her friend a smile, which was not returned. Miss Millington's eyebrows were rising towards her hairline and her eyes had become rather rounded, as though she believed that she was giving Deborah the option to escape from a difficult situation, but Deborah merely smiled. "I will stay in sight of my mother, however."

Assuring her friend a little more, she then turned and walked slowly with Lord Brookmire further along the path.

"You say that you will see Lady Yardley this evening."

Lord Brookmire's voice was low, falling immediately into conversation with her as they walked together. Deborah nodded, her heart quickening a little as she glanced to where her arm now wound through his.

"Yes, I shall see her this evening. I cannot be sure whether she is here in the park at present, although she may be." Deborah glanced across at Lord Brookmire, noticing how his hair glistened with bronze and copper as the sun shone upon it. "Are you to attend Lord Brathwaite's soiree?"

Lord Brookmire dropped his head low.

"I dare not." He would not look at her. "I have been directed by Lord Anderton to do something truly dreadful and quite frankly, I am going to remain in my townhouse so that I might attempt to think through what is to be done. I wanted to speak with you and Lady Yardley also, in the hope that one of us could come up with a solution to this difficulty."

She slowed her steps, glancing over her shoulder to where her mother still stood talking with Lord Anderton. She caught her eye, but Lady Prescott did not respond with any sort of surprise in seeing Deborah arm in arm with Lord Brookmire.

"What is it that Lord Anderton has said? Did he approach you in the park?"

Lord Brookmire nodded.

"He has not delayed, for he is quite frustrated that his plan as regarded Lord Williamston and Lady Jemima has been foiled. Therefore, he has stated that I must not fail this time. I protested that I had not had the opportunity to either fail or succeed the last time, but he would not hear of it." Deborah pressed his arm a little, hearing the frustration flutter through his voice. To her, his frame was rather tense but much to her astonishment, his free hand came to settle on hers as they walked together. "Do not think that I have forgotten how much I owe to your generous and compassionate heart." Lord Brookmire came to a complete stop, looking at her now, his eyes meeting hers. "I am all too aware of my behavior and how quickly and keenly you have been willing to set the past aside. Even now, your sympathy and support is something which I certainly do not merit but value greatly."

Fearful of what he would see in her eyes, Deborah quickly turned her head, her eyes to the path.

"Thank you, Lord Brookmire," she said quickly, all too aware of how furiously her heart was pounding. "What is it that you must do for Lord Anderton?"

A harsh laugh broke from Lord Brookmire's lips.

"I believe that he is testing my loyalty. You may not know of it, but Lord Marchmont is a dear friend of mine. I have spoken to you of how he warned me repeatedly over my reputation, and thereafter about Lord Anderton. In my foolish stubbornness, I refused to listen to him, and I now find myself deeply regretting that. Had I only listened to him, then I might not find myself in this circumstance."

Deborah caught her breath, realizing what Lord Brookmire meant.

"Lord Anderton has spoken of something you must do against Lord Marchmont."

Lord Brookmire nodded, his gaze catching hers again. His face had paled a little, his lips flat, although his jaw was forward, perhaps hiding the anger which must now be flooding through him.

"As I say, I believe that Lord Anderton is testing my loyalty. He wants to see how much power he has over me, and whether I will do whatever I must. Either I will protect my reputation, or I will protect my friend." Deborah bit her tongue, refusing to ask any more questions and giving Lord Brookmire a chance to explain further. After a heavy breath, he did continue, and Deborah's heart ached as he explained. "There is an evening next week which is open to gentlemen only. It is by invitation from Lord Dalton and consists of gambling and cards." Lord Brookmire sighed, shaking his head "I must play against Lord Marchmont, for he is a gentleman who enjoys gambling on occasion. He is rather good at it and certainly does win a great deal, but he is also a gentleman not inclined towards too much liquor which must aid him a great deal. Lord Anderton states that I am not only to ply him with brandy, but I am also to cheat during our gambling game and take as much from him as I possibly can."

"Oh." Deborah closed her eyes tightly as Lord Brookmire's steps came to a stop once more. "How dreadful. Can you not speak to Lord Marchmont and warn him?"

Lord Brookmire shook his head.

"Lord Anderton warned me that he is always aware of

my actions, and I have no doubt that he will have other gentlemen watching me. No doubt they will be blackmailed into doing so in the same way as I am, but all the same, they will report to Lord Anderton should they see me in discussion with Lord Marchmont before the evening takes place. Any warning I give him will be noted, and I fear then that Lord Anderton will reveal all to the Marquess of Harrogate."

Hearing the concern in his voice, Deborah's only urge was to relieve his worry a little. Lifting her chin, she offered him a brief smile, keeping her voice steady and wishing that she might do more than simply speak words of comfort.

"Do not fear, Lord Brookmire. Surely we will simply tell Lord Marchmont of what is to take place."

"If only you could." Lord Brookmire looked away. "But Lord Marchmont may not then play at all, and Lord Anderton will know that I have warned him... but yet something must be done. I do not know what we can do, but the last thing I wish for is to betray or injure my friend."

Deborah's sympathy for him grew rapidly, like a flower blooming after a rain shower.

"It is good to hear you speak so, Lord Brookmire," she said gently "You have an allegiance to your friend. You have great concern for him, and I am sure that, were he aware of it, he would be grateful indeed."

Lord Brookmire dropped his head.

"You do not know how much he has endured from me. I am all the more ashamed of how little I listened to him."

Swallowing hard, and knowing that her mother would wish her very soon to end her conversation with Lord Brookmire, Deborah took a small step forward. Finding his hand, she pressed it gently, then dropped his fingers before her entire body could heat to the point where she felt enveloped into flame.

"I will speak to Lady Yardley this evening," she promised. "I am certain that, between us, we can find a way for you to escape again from Lord Anderton."

His gaze lifted to hers, a small wry smile touching the edge of his mouth.

"I do trust you, Miss Madeley," he murmured, "for I have no one else to turn to."

CHAPTER TEN

"What can be done?" Deborah began to pace up and down Lady Yardley's drawing room, driven to the movement by frustration and concern. Some of her friends were present also - Lady Elizabeth, Miss Millington, and Lady Sherbourne – and all watched her with such wide eyes and surprised expressions that Deborah paused in her walk, realizing that she had barely explained herself.

"Forgive me. I know that you think of Lord Brookmire as a scoundrel, for that has been his reputation. But he approached Lady Yardley with a request and, given her consideration of the matter, I find I am in complete agreement with her. Lord Brookmire is now a gentleman seeking to reform himself." Her words were tumbling over each other in an effort to be heard. "There is to be a gambling evening for the gentlemen of London soon, held at Lord Dalton's townhouse. Lord Brookmire is to attend, but Lord Anderton has blackmailed him into doing something quite dreadful. He is to ply one of his close friends, Lord Marchmont, with liquor – and, being a gentleman who does not very often take liquor, it will have a hasty effect! Thereafter, Lord Brookmire is to make certain that he cheats his way into taking a great deal of wealth from Lord Marchmont."

She paused for a moment, tilting her head in the hope that some wonderful idea would strike her, then flung up her hands. "I do not know what we are to do. If Lord Marchmont is warned in any way, then Lord Brookmire fears Lord Anderton will know the truth of it."

"Lord Anderton." Miss Millington was frowning, hard. "What has Lord Anderton to do with this?"

"Lord Anderton is blackmailing Lord Brookmire." Lady Yardley's calm voice interrupted Deborah's frantic explanations. "We do not need to go into the reason why, but needless to say, Lord Anderton is proving himself to be very much a rogue in this matter. He is the villain here, and we must find a way to protect Lord Marchmont whilst at the same time, making certain that he is entirely unaware of the situation."

"But how are we to do so?" Again, Deborah began to walk up and down the drawing room, her mind twirling as it had been, ever since Lord Brookmire had spoken to her. "We are ladies - therefore we are not invited to this evening of gambling and cards." Her eyes closed, and she stopped suddenly, rubbing one hand across her forehead. "I confess that I cannot see a way to aid the gentleman. I do not doubt that Lord Anderton will make certain that Lord Marchmont becomes aware that Lord Brookmire cheated him and, upon learning of it, I have no doubt that his anger will be directed solely towards Lord Brookmire. Lord Brookmire will be unable to tell him the truth, and thus their friendship will be at an end. Lord Marchmont, in the meantime, will lose a great deal of coin and yes, Lord Brookmire might seek to return it but, even if he were to do so, the damage will have been done. Lord Brookmire's reputation as a scoundrel will become fixed, even to those he considered his friends."

Lady Yardley rose from her chair, walked across the room, and took Deborah's hand.

"Come and sit down, else you will quite fatigue yourself!" Leading her to a chair, she smiled gently as she took her own seat again. "Yes, you are correct that we have not been invited to the gambling evening, but that is where the Ledger is to be used." Lady Yardley paused for a moment, then lifted both shoulders. "I believe that my own husband, as well as Lady Sherbourne's husband, have been invited to the evening. We can take *them* into our confidence, are we not?"

Deborah pressed her lips hard together, trying not to ask questions, just to let Lady Yardley speak, but she could not hold it back.

"Might I ask what good it will do to have them there? Lord Brookmire will be forced to do as he has been instructed, regardless."

"Yes, that is true." Lady Yardley tipped her head, still thinking. "But if we use the Ledger to make certain that the invitation is open to more gentlemen than just those who have already been invited, then there may be a chance that some other rascals take their place at the tables. It may not then be only Lord Brookmire who is considered to be cheating."

Deborah's shoulders loosened, her tension beginning to be chased away by Lady Yardley's suggestion.

"Perhaps Lord Yardley or Lord Sherbourne could point out other gentlemen who were cheating, rather than only

Lord Brookmire?"

Lady Yardley nodded slowly.

"Yes. I could make certain that Lord Yardley takes with him to the table one who has the reputation of being something of a cheat. It might take a little planning, but I am sure that my husband could do such a thing. He will have to be told of it all, of course. I do not keep any secrets from him."

Deborah nodded fervently, her fingers clenching and unclenching into tight fists.

"Do you think that it will succeed? Another gentleman will cheat before Lord Brookmire is required to?"

Lady Sherbourne's eyes lit up.

"More than that!" she exclaimed, speaking hurriedly. "What if they were to demand that no liquor be drunk at the table? It would be unexpected, certainly, but my husband could demand that there be no brandy nor whisky served, so that every gentleman keeps a clear head. That would make certain that it was not Lord Brookmire's doing when he could not offer brandy to Lord Marchmont, for it would be at my husband's request."

The dark clouds, which had been surrounding Deborah for many an hour, began to break apart as she looked first at Lady Sherbourne and then at Lady Yardley.

"Do you think such a thing would work?"

"I think it is the only chance we have." Lady Yardley lifted both shoulders. "I know you are deeply concerned, but we must explain the plan to all three gentlemen, and thereafter hope that it all goes as we wish. I would warn you to be cautious." Reaching across, she squeezed Deborah's hand for a moment. "Lord Anderton is always watching. I am certain that he has others who watch for him, and they may very well be aware of the amount of time Lord Brookmire spends in your company. It is not that I think they would have any suspicion that you were involved in the whole affair, but rather that they might seek to use you against Lord Brookmire."

"Do you think Deborah might be in danger from being in Lord Brookmire's company?"

Miss Millington's eyes were wide, but Lady Yardley quickly shook her head.

"No. It is not Lord Brookmire who is at fault in this, although, had he not done certain things then he would not find himself in this situation – but now he is at the mercy of Lord Anderton. I do not think that I have ever heard of a more calculating fellow than he."

Her eyes flashed for a moment and Deborah's stomach twisted suddenly. She did not think that she could step away from Lord Brookmire's company, not even if she were instructed to by her mother. Even the thought brought her too much pain... but she dared not say a word about her feelings to any one of her friends, or even to Lady Yardley.

"I understand." She managed a small smile "Thank you, Lady Yardley, I will write to Lord Brookmire and state that a meeting will be arranged very soon."

"Of course." Lady Yardley smiled. "Tell Lord Brookmire to call upon me tomorrow afternoon, if he pleases. You may be present also, if you wish."

Deborah nodded; her mind already on the letter she would write. When Lady Yardley offered her the use of the library to write the letter immediately, Deborah accepted the chance at once. Hurrying from the room and into the silence of the hall, she drew in a deep breath, letting relief flow through her. She had to pray that this plan would succeed and that, yet again, Lord Anderton's cruelties would be prevented before they could even begin.

Making her way to the library, Deborah stopped

suddenly at the sight of the very gentleman she had been thinking of, walking down the hallway toward her. The butler was walking ahead of him, no doubt intending to lead him to Lady Yardley and announce him but, upon seeing her, Lord Brookmire turned his steps towards her. The butler melted away into the shadows as Deborah quickly bobbed a curtsey.

"Lord Brookmire."

Much to her embarrassment, her hand reached out for him by instinct, and she pulled it back sharply, praying that he had not noticed.

"Miss Madeley." His hands going behind his back, Lord Brookmire bowed to her. "I was just going to speak with Lady Yardley. How good it is to see you."

His compliment made her blush.

"Thank you, Lord Brookmire. Can I ask if something more has happened?"

Lord Brookmire looked away.

"No. I come to seek her wisdom. I confess, I am over-whelmed as I look back upon my life and see how dread-fully I have acted in the past. I thought that it would be wise to speak to someone who, from the very start, has told me that they hope that this experience will give me the oppor-tunity to change."

He dropped his gaze and shuffled his feet as if there were something more he wanted to say but, after a few moments, it was clear that no further remark was to come from him.

Deborah smiled at him. How different he was to the gentleman she had first met, the gentleman who had laughed and teased and been overly confident, who had been determined to prove to her that he would have his way regardless!

"I am sure that Lady Yardley will be more than willing to speak with you but, from my perspective, I do see a great difference in you already." Again, she reached out, but this time she pressed his hand for a moment, not pulling it back as she had done before. "Lady Yardley is to be admired, for she certainly has a great deal of wisdom within her, wisdom that she is more than happy to share."

Lord Brookmire chuckled, but there was no happiness within the sound.

"I wish I had taken heed of such wisdom before now." He shrugged his shoulders, then straightened them. "However, do not allow my reflections to hold you back from your task. Was there somewhere you were going?"

A slight flush edged its way up into Deborah's cheeks as she laughed.

"I was to go to the library and write you a short note, but since you are here, you have saved me from that task."

Lord Brookmire grinned, his green eyes busy with a burst of sudden laughter.

"Then I am glad to have interrupted you," he answered, his smile sending lightning through Deborah's veins. "What is it that you were to write to me? I should have been very glad to have received a note from you. I am sure it would have lifted my spirits."

The heat within her now turned into a furnace, and Deborah quickly pulled her eyes from his face, finding herself unable to hold his gaze steadily. She felt too much when she was looking into his eyes and, no doubt, her words would soon become incomprehensible if she kept gazing into his face.

"It is about the gambling evening." Looking over his shoulder, she managed to smile, praying that he could not hear the thump of her heart which, to her, seemed overwhelmingly loud. "Lady Yardley has come up with a plan for how we might make certain that Lord Marchmont escapes from Lord Anderton's endeavor."

His swift catch of breath had her looking back at him, seeing his eyes widen.

"Truly? What is it that she plans to do?"

Lord Brookmire had stepped closer in obvious anticipation, and Deborah's awareness of how near he now stood to her stole her words away for some moments. Instead of responding, she simply looked back into his eyes, seeing the shards of emerald amongst a forest of leaves and shrubs. It was not until he smiled at her that she found her voice, her face hot with embarrassment.

"Yes, Lady Yardley. She..." Closing her eyes, she took in a steadying breath. "Lady Yardley is to ask her husband – and Lady Sherbourne the same – to be of aid to you. They are both to attend and will sit at the same table as you and Lord Marchmont, bringing with them gentlemen who are known to cheat at cards. In addition, Lord Sherbourne will insist that no liquor is permitted at the table so that heads might be kept quite clear for the game. During the game, Lord Yardley and Lord Sherbourne will keep watch and will, we hope, catch whoever has cheated long before you are required to." Lifting one shoulder, she smiled a little ruefully. "It is risky, of course," she finished, seeing how his eyes shuttered for a moment. "There is no guarantee that another gentleman *will* cheat, but we must hope that one will do so, particularly if he is known for it."

To her surprise, Lord Brookmire ran one hand over his forehead, dropping his head low as though he did not agree with this plan. She waited for him to speak, to make his concerns known, only for his hands to find hers, his fingers curling around her own as he let out a long, slow breath.

"Once more, it seems, I am to be shown a kindness which I do not deserve." There were shadows about his eyes, as though a single word of harshness from her might break his spirit entirely. "I do not know what to say."

"There's a good deal of kindness in this world, I think." Murmuring softly, she tilted her head, regarding him carefully. "Kindness comes in many forms. Lord Sherbourne and Lord Yardley do not want Lord Anderton to be successful with his schemes. As I have said, there is still something of a risk, but I must hope that their plans will be successful."

Lord Brookmire nodded.

"Thank you, Miss Madeley." He let out another breath, then smiled. "I am grateful. Lord Sherbourne and Lord Yardley would have every right and reason to stay far away from me, given my reputation, but now here they are, willing to do whatever they can to save me from my own foolishness and, by doing so, to save my friend also."

An overpowering desire to throw her arms around his neck and pull herself close to him enveloped her, so strongly that Deborah had to suck in air, clench her fists, curl her toes in her shoes, and press her lips tightly together so that she remained precisely where she was. She believed him. She believed his every word. He was not, as she had first considered, saying such things simply to garner her consideration. Instead, he was truly aware of his past sins and was slowly coming to realize what sort of gentleman that had made him. It had not seemed to be at all concerning to him before but now, his expression spoke of a brokenness which she believed would lead to an entire renewal of his character.

"And what is it that I am to do?"

"Absolutely nothing." Deborah smiled quickly, relieved

that she had been able to contain herself. "Lord Anderton will, no doubt, be watching you, making certain that you have done as you are asked and you must make attempts to follow his directives. Do just as Lord Anderton expects. If, however, as we hope, his plans are thwarted by gentlemen other than yourself, then I have no doubt that he will not be able to place the blame upon you... no matter how much he might wish to do so."

Lord Brookmire smiled at her, his fingers squeezing hers again. Did he have even an inkling of the swell of emotion which rose within her as he held her hand in his? Did he know just how much she had to steel herself against being overcome by it?

"I am once again brought low by the generosity and kind-heartedness of others." Lord Brookmire set his shoulders, then tilted his head a little. "I shall speak with Lady Yardley now and express the same sentiment to her. Do you intend to return to her company also?"

She laughed.

"Indeed, for now that I do not need to write to you, I suppose I have every reason to return."

Chuckling, he then offered her his arm, releasing her hand as he did so.

"Then might you wish to walk with me?"

The butler stepped out of a nearby room as though he had somehow known that they were preparing to return to Lady Yardley, and after a quick look in Lord Brookmire's direction, began to lead them both back towards the parlor. With a smile. Deborah took Lord Brookmire's arm and as she walked alongside him, her heart filled with such happiness, it was as though everything else which had come before was dull and grey in comparison to this moment. It appeared as though Lord Brookmire was becoming rather dear to her heart. She could not hide that truth from herself any longer and, the more she considered it, the more Deborah realized that she had no wish to.

CHAPTER ELEVEN

"Good evening."

Phillip managed to smile, though the tension which ran through him forced it away rather quickly.

"Good evening, Lord Dalton."

His host for the evening grinned broadly, shaking Phillip's hand firmly.

"I am very glad to see you. It looks to be an excellent evening, does it not?" Phillip nodded but said nothing, clasping his hands behind his back so that he would pull his shoulders back rather than lifting them too high, which revealed his tension. "There are more tables in the library, Lord Brookmire," Lord Dalton chuckled. "It seems as though my wife, in her eagerness to support my endeavor, asked Lady Yardley to place a notice in 'The London Ledger' that I was to have an evening of cards and the like. I was forced, therefore, to have many other tables set up for the evening, for it seems I shall have a good many more gentlemen here than I had anticipated." He smiled broadly. "I hope this evening is an excellent time for all."

"I am sure it shall be."

Deeply relieved that, in that regard, there had been significant success in Lady Yardley's endeavor thus far, Phillip looked around the room and caught sight of none other than Lord Yardley and Lord Sherbourne. They were standing together, smiling, and as he caught their eye, Lord Yardley inclined his head but did nothing more. Phillip understood why for, after all, he did not want Lord Anderton, who was also present, to be aware that they were known to each other, or to become suspicious that they had colluded with respect to this evening's activities. He made his way forward and spoke to one or two other gentlemen, only for Lord Marchmont to appear by his side.

"Good evening." His friend smiled at him. "I suppose I should not be surprised in the least to see you here. You will, no doubt, have a pleasant evening, I am sure."

Phillip tried to smile, anxious now that, despite their endeavor, Lord Marchmont would find himself suffering by Phillip's hand.

"I am sure that I will enjoy myself as I always do."

"Although I will say," Lord Marchmont said, studying Phillip with a suddenly severe eye. "You have not been behaving as I had thought you might." His eyes flashed for a moment. "I do not mean to say that you are not a rogue, but rather that you have not been displaying any such behaviors of late."

Not knowing whether to be pleased or embarrassed that his friend had noticed such a thing, Phillip hesitated before he replied, throwing out both hands.

"Mayhap I have decided to listen to your warnings after all."

It was a minimal explanation, but it was one that Lord

Marchmont seemed to accept, for he smiled widely and then slapped Phillip on the shoulder.

"Well, if that is true, I am very glad to hear it." His hand fell back to his side. "Might I also say that I have seen you often in company with one particular young lady, recently?"

Phillip's eyes flared with sudden alarm, only for Lord Marchmont to chuckle.

"You need not fear that I shall judge you, nor warn you away from her. It is only to note aloud that I am pleased to see you thinking so highly of only one young lady that you then draw near only to her... particularly when she pushed you away so quickly at the beginning of your acquaintance!"

Phillip immediately shook his head.

"Do not think well of me for it." He put one hand to his heart. "I do believe that, had not certain circumstances taken place, I would have continued in my roguish ways." Seeing Lord Marchmont's eyes flare, he looked away, unwilling to speak of his struggles at present. "But yes, I suppose in a way, it is a good thing for this particular situation to have taken hold, for it has allowed me to see the consequences of my previous behaviors."

Lord Marchmont nodded slowly, but held Phillip's gaze in silence for some moments, perhaps waiting for Phillip to say something more. Phillip did not wish to disclose anything about Lord Anderton, not at this juncture, and thus, he simply shook his head.

"Well, whatever difficulties it is you speak of, I hope that they resolve themselves quickly." Lord Marchmont offered him a small smile "If you are to find happiness with Miss Madeley, then I wish you success in that endeavor also."

A somewhat broken laugh came from Phillip.

"I am entirely certain that Lord Prescott will be more than disinclined to accept me, should I seek to court his daughter." It was not a thought he had given much consideration to of late, but now that Lord Marchmont had noticed his interest in Miss Madeley, it was something that Phillip had to consider. "I will not pretend that I am not affected by her, though I do not permit myself to think much of it."

Lord Marchmont shrugged.

"Well, perhaps, if you continue along this path, Lord Prescott might be a little more open to considering you," he suggested, making Phillip smile. "It may take time, but I am sure that, if you prove yourself - and if Miss Madeley is keen for your company also – and she certainly appears to be for she is not pushing you away– then mayhap you do have some hope after all."

Before Phillip could say anything more, they were then called to the tables, and Phillip glanced to where Lord Yardley, and Lord Sherbourne stood. Seeing them edge their way to the table in the corner, he suggested to Lord Marchmont that they move to the same one. With a nod, Lord Marchmont made his way toward the table, with Phillip following. There were already a few gentlemen seated and Phillip greeted each one by name, treating Lord Sherbourne and Lord Yardley the same as the others, so that he would not make more of their presence. A glance over his shoulder told him that Lord Anderton was now in the drawing room, but was doing nothing other than wandering around the tables, showing no obvious intention of sitting down at any of them.

"Are you not to join us Lord Anderton?" Lord Sherbourne grinned as Lord Anderton strolled towards them. "It is an evening of card playing, is it not? I have heard by reputation that you enjoy an evening such as this!"

Lord Anderton laughed, but shook his head.

"Yes, that is true, but this evening I think I shall watch the first few games before I seat myself." Laughing again, he tilted his head. "Alas, I am a little fatigued after a night of some excess," he confessed, forcing a smile that did not touch his eyes. "I am sure you will not mind if I watch, however?"

"No, of course not," another gentleman replied, looking a little relieved that Lord Anderton was not to join them.

Phillip said nothing, sitting in his seat and aware of his chest tightening at just how close Lord Anderton would be to him.

The face of Miss Madeley came into his mind, and Phillip took a deep breath, finding just the thought of her to be a comfort. What was it she had said to him?

Do just as Lord Anderton expects.

That was all he was to do. He was to behave just as Lord Anderton anticipated and that meant suggesting that liquor be placed upon the table, setting out a glass before Lord Marchmont, and making certain it was always full. Thereafter, he was to attempt to cheat in whatever way he could, in the hope that his other companions would not be aware of him doing so. In addition, he was to focus his attempts on Lord Marchmont, to try to steal as much coin from him as he could. Whether or not the endeavors to force this plan into failure would be successful, Phillip did not know, but he prayed it would be as they hoped.

"Are we quite ready?" Lord Sutton looked around the table, grinning widely as the gentlemen nodded. "Then shall we deal the cards?"

"Wait a moment." Waving one hand, he garnered the attention of the others at the table. "Before we begin, would anyone like a glass of something to calm their nerves?" He forced a chuckle. "Lord Dalton has some excellent French brandy and some very fine whisky also." More than a few gentlemen agreed and said that yes, they would like a glass, but Lord Marchmont shook his head. "Come now, Marchmont! A little glass will do you good."

Phillip grinned and slapped his friend on the shoulder, all the while hating his falsehood. No doubt Lord Anderton was crowing inwardly, delighted with what Phillip was being forced to do.

"I should agree with Lord Marchmont. I do not think *any* liquor at all is advisable." Lord Yardley cleared his throat, then shrugged as the others looked at him. "I would advise, in fact, that we keep the table clear of such things. It would ensure that we all keep our thoughts quite clear. Given that there is to be a large amount of gaming this evening and no doubt some high wagering, I think it would be for the best if we did not confound ourselves by imbibing."

"I quite agree." Lord Sherbourne nodded. "We should have no brandy or whisky at this table. That means that anyone who loses will not be able to blame liquor for their failure." Chuckling, he nudged Lord Yardley. "Lord Yardley has been known to use such an excuse before, and I am disinclined to have him complain about it again."

Given that both Lord Yardley and Lord Sherbourne were highly respected gentlemen of the *ton,* most of the other gentlemen at the table immediately began to agree with them. Inwardly delighted, Phillip placed a frown on his face and attempted to protest, seeing Lord Anderton watching the goings-on with narrowed eyes.

"Alas, it seems as though you are in the minority, Lord Brookmire." Lord Sutton grinned as Phillip rolled his eyes. "Those at this table shall be not allowed either bandy or whisky. We shall play with clear heads and strong minds. That, I think, is a very wise idea from Lord Yardley and Lord Sherbourne. So shall we now begin our game?"

Phillip looked to Lord Anderton, shrugging in what he hoped was a nonchalant fashion, but Lord Anderton's face was already dark with anger. There was nothing Phillip could do, for even if he had truly wished to imbibe, Lord Sherbourne and Lord Yardley's protests would have prevented him from doing so. Relieved that this one requirement had been taken from him, Phillip then set his mind to the game.

The game went very well at first. Phillip made no move to cheat, for it would be much too obvious so early in the game. Soon, however, he began to notice that there was something amiss. Glancing around the table, he took in one gentleman after the other, attempting to work out who it was that was adding an extra card here or there. He could not quite understand it, and certainly could not see the person responsible as yet, but it was with utter relief that he accepted that someone else was playing unfairly. Whichever gentlemen Lord Yardley and Lord Sherbourne had brought to the table, one of them was already on their way to doing exactly as Phillip had been tasked to do. The game continued for some time and Phillip, casting a glance to Lord Anderton, saw him smiling. Of course, he realized, Lord Anderton would think that *he* was the one doing such a thing but, before he could do or say a word to anyone, Lord Sutton let out a loud exclamation.

"It *is* you, Lord Norville." Bending over the side of his chair, he picked up a card from the floor, and then brandished it at Lord Norville, who had gone very pale indeed. "I wondered who was taking an extra card now and again, but I see that it is you! How dare you do such a thing?"

This loud exclamation had almost everyone else in the room looking at Lord Norville and Phillip sat back in his chair, watching as Lord Anderton's smile slid slowly from his face. It was not Phillip who was to be blamed for the cheating then, but rather, Lord Norville. Given that Phillip had not as yet even begun to think about doing anything untoward, it was all the more delightful to him to see Lord Anderton lose yet again.

"I am not going to play this game any longer." Lord Sherbourne slammed his cards down on the table and then got up, placing both hands on either side as he glared across the table at Lord Norville. "You are a trickster, Lord Norville. You are attempting to cheat us all by playing in a most unfair manner. How dare you call yourself a gentleman and behave so?"

At first, the gentleman protested, only then to sink low in his chair as the other gentlemen rose, one by one, from the table. Phillip too got to his feet, unable to keep the grin plastered across his face from revealing itself. He caught one or two odd glances and scrubbed one hand over his features, trying to remove it.

"Might I suggest that we all move to separate tables." It was not Lord Yardley, Lord Sherbourne, Lord Marchmont nor Phillip who spoke, but another gentleman entirely. "Each one of us should go to join another game so that we split our table up and, as a consequence, Lord Norville is left without the chance to play with any of us." He gestured to Phillip. "Lord Brookmire, why do you not join Lord Litton's game in the library?"

He continued to direct the gentlemen, one to each of the other tables, and Phillip smiled in relief as Lord Marchmont was kept in the drawing room at another table. With a broad smile on his face, he made his way out of the room and towards the library, overwhelmed with satisfaction that yet again, Lord Anderton's plans had been quite spoiled. There was no obvious way for Lord Anderton to place the blame upon Phillip's shoulders, for now another gentleman had directed every person to another table, which meant that Lord Anderton could only blame bad luck.

"At least you tried to do what I had asked of you this time."

Phillip swung around quickly as Lord Anderton followed him into the hallway.

"I did." He kept his shoulders straight, his chin lifting as Lord Anderton sneered at him as though he had meant his previous remark as a jest. "It seems as though fate is set against me injuring the lives and fortunes of others."

Lord Anderton rolled his eyes, silently stating that he found Phillip's remark foolish.

"Have no doubt, I will find something else for you. Something where you shall have to succeed regardless of the actions of others."

"Or you could forget about the entire matter." Phillip spread out his hands to either side ."Just leave this as it stands, Lord Anderton. I have done nothing to injure you and you know very well that I only do as you ask under duress."

"It is true that you have not hurt me," Lord Anderton replied quickly, "but I am a gentleman looking for an advantage, and you, I am afraid, are very much someone I can use to my advantage. I like to keep my hands clean, to make sure that none in society know the truth of me - evidence of that you have seen for yourself, given that you had very little idea of my true character when I proposed that wager to you." His smile curled around his lips, but it was not one which Phillip liked. "Might I suggest, Lord Brookmire, that you have underestimated me? You did not see the depth of my character before, and even though you see it now, you still think that there will be some goodness in me, something that will prevent me from continuing down this path. I can assure you that there is not."

His heart sinking slowly from the giddy heights it had reached only a few moments ago, Phillip let his hands drop to his sides.

"Perhaps *this* is something that I am glad of Lord Anderton," he responded slowly, letting his words hang in the air between them. "I have been saved from becoming like you. I believe, if I had continued as I had intended, then perhaps, even as early as the end of this Season, I would have been as cold, as cruel, and as calculating as you." A slight shudder ran through him. "I would rather be a gentleman who is attempting to redeem themselves rather than a gentleman who has no true companions, or compassion."

An ugly look smeared itself across Lord Anderton's face, rendering his expression a dark scowl, his eyes pinpricks as he narrowed them, heat in his cheeks and his lip curling furiously. He took a step closer, one pudgy hand curling into a fist.

"How dare you speak to me so? You know nothing about my life, and speak only in an attempt to push yourself into a position of power."

Boldly, Phillip continued without hesitation – for what was it that the gentleman could do against Phillip's words?

"That is not true, Lord Anderton. I watch you, and I see the truth of you, as you have said. You are someone who has no true friends. Everyone is either afraid of you, or seeks to be near you simply because of what you can offer them. No young lady is ever eager to spend time in your company, and they do, in fact, shy away from you as though they can see in your eyes the sort of heart you carry within you. I can see now, Lord Anderton, and I know that, in you forcing my hand, I have gained good things."

Lord Anderton laughed mockingly.

"I hardly believe that."

Phillip continued, undaunted by the interruption or the mockery he heard in Lord Anderton's voice.

"It is true, whether you believe it or not. I have gained closer friendships with those who were already my friends, and I have found myself realizing the comfort it can be to tie oneself to another, rather than pursuing the many. I have the consideration of others, I have some respect from those I consider my equals, and those both above and below my standing. Mothers are no longer as eager to pull their daughters away from me, gentlemen do not turn their back upon me. The more I reflect upon the gentleman I was, and the gentleman I wish to be, the more I desire the latter... and it is *you* who has given me that. It is only a pity that you cannot see it."

He did not give Lord Anderton time to answer, but turned sharply and began to walk to the library again. He had expected Lord Anderton to rebuff him, to say something which would bring him pain, or to shoot back a dark response but instead, the only sound was his footsteps on the hall floor as he strode away.

CHAPTER TWELVE

"Miss Madeley."

The moment Lord Brookmire said her name, Deborah's whole body flooded with light. She turned sharply, her hand reaching out for him as Lord Brookmire's fingers found hers. Relieved that they were in the shadows at the side of the ballroom, Deborah pressed his hand firmly, a smile spreading across her face as Lord Brookmire grinned at her.

"Before you ask, yes, the evening was successful." His free hand ran over his eyes, but his smile remained. "I did nothing whatsoever but, needless to say, I was able to escape from Lord Anderton's demands as a result of the aid of Lord Yardley and Lord Sherbourne... as well as Lord Norville's greed!"

Her heart slammed hard against her ribs as her eyes flew wide.

"Then another gentleman dared to cheat?"

Lord Brookmire nodded.

"I spoke briefly to Lord Sherbourne later in the evening. He assured me that the gentlemen both he and Lord

Yardley encouraged to the table were all known to be inclined towards cheating at one time or another." Chuckling softly, he shrugged, and Deborah pressed her other hand to her heart, joyous with relief.

"How glad I am to hear it."

"As I was to see it!"

She laughed, then finally released his hand and threw a glance over her shoulder to make certain that her mother had not noticed. Lady Prescott was only a few steps away but her back was turned towards Deborah as she remained in deep conversation with another lady.

"I confess, I was very worried indeed for you, all last evening. I barely slept for fear of what might have taken place! I am relieved to hear that Lord Marchmont has been spared any difficulty and that your friendship has not been ruined."

Noticing how Lord Brookmire's eyes searched her face, and seeing his gentle smile directed solely towards her, caused a blush to warm her cheeks. The emotions he brought up in her were becoming more severe every time he simply *looked* at her, every time he was near. It was as though her heart threw itself into a tumult of exultation and delight. How could it be that the gentleman she had despised, the gentleman she had demanded silently she stay away from, was now the only one she wanted close to her?

"Might I..." Lord Brookmire looked away suddenly, rubbing one hand over his chin. "Mayhap it is much too presumptuous of me, but I was hoping that you might have a dance card that I could...?" Squeezing his eyes closed, he let out a long breath. "It seems, Miss Madeley, as though your presence encourages my words to throw themselves around so that they come out quite tangled!"

The excitement and anticipation now flooding her had

Deborah ready to dance where she stood. Was he really asking her to dance? The thought of being in his arms had her skin burning hot and, without a word, she slipped her dance card from her wrist and handed it to him. With a jolt, she recalled that she had not asked her mother if she and Lord Brookmire could stand up together, but all the same, Deborah's heart would not allow her to refuse him.

"Miss Madeley?"

Lord Brookmire looked at her dance card, a small frown dancing across his forehead.

"Were you asking whether or not you might sign my dance card? If you wish to do so, then my answer would be yes."

She held it out to him, seeing how his eyes flew to hers, rounding gently. Embarrassment flew through her and she dropped her hand, suddenly mortified. Perhaps she had been presumptuous. Perhaps Lord Brookmire had not been about to ask her to dance!

"My dear Miss Madeley." The gentle tenderness in his voice had her embarrassment fading. "Pray, do not mistake my hesitation for disinclination. It is only that I did not expect you to be so willing."

Deborah said nothing, swallowing the tightness in her throat. For what was there for her to say, as regarded this willingness? It was not as though she could tell him that the reason for her eagerness was because of how deeply her emotions swirled whenever she thought of him. She could not express to him the thrill which flitted through her at the thought of being in his arms. Whatever dance it was he chose, whether it be the quadrille, the country dance, or even the waltz, she could hardly wait to be close to him.

"I would have taken your waltz were it not for fear that your mother would refuse." With a smile, he handed back her dance card. "The cotillion, I think, and thereafter the polka, if you are quite contented with that."

Blinking rapidly, she looked at her dance card carefully, a little surprised to see that there were two dances where his initials were placed.

"Two dances."

She said such a thing without any real awareness and it was only when Lord Brookmire's eyes flared that she attempted to explain herself.

"I am not at all upset by it, Lord Brookmire, it is only that I am a little surprised. You are kind enough to ask to dance with me, but to dance twice together..."

Did he know the significance of what he had done? Her eyes held his and, after a moment, Lord Brookmire moved a little closer.

"I hope you know just how much you have come to mean to me." His breath ran lightly across her cheek, as though it were a gentle touch from his hand, and she shivered lightly. "I admire you greatly, Miss Madeley. I find that your compassion, your willing spirit, and your sweetness have taken hold of me. I struggle to think of anyone I admire more than you."

His confession was so utterly astonishing, that his words froze her in position. Her feet were anchored to the floor, her hands stuck to her sides, and her eyes fixed on his. There would have been a time when she would have doubted his words to be genuine, but now, as she looked at him, she could tell that there was no guile there upon his lips. Was it possible that he was feeling as she did? Could it be that his heart held the same feelings as her own? And if it was so, then what was she to do with it? Did it mean that she might find herself one day taking tea with him? That *he* would be the one she would walk alongside in the park? The thought of such a thing made her smile and, on seeing it, Lord Brookmire lifted his eyebrow in question. Laughing, she dropped her head quickly, a little embarrassed.

"I do hope this gentleman is not bothering you, Miss Madeley."

The warmth between herself and Lord Brookmire faded as Deborah forced a smile, turning towards Lord Cleverley, catching the frown on his face, and noting how his eyes narrowed as he looked at Lord Brookmire. A little irritated by his arrival – for, inadvertently, he had interrupted what had been a very pleasant, if somewhat confusing moment with Lord Brookmire – she shook her head.

"No, indeed, not, Lord Cleverley." Lord Cleverley looked at her, one eyebrow lifting in question. "Lord Brookmire was simply signing my dance card."

Lord Cleverley's eyes flew wide, his breath catching in an audible gasp.

"You do not mean to say that you will stand up with him?"

"I had thought I would, yes."

Deborah turned her attention toward Lord Cleverley, lifting first one eyebrow and then the other as Lord Cleverley's mouth dropped open.

"I considered you many things, Miss Madeley, but I certainly did not think you unwise."

Deborah released a small chuckle, unable to keep it back. It was not a sound of mirth, however, but rather of frustration that he should think to speak to her so. He was not her parent, not her companion or guardian. Why should he think of himself as having any right to dictate who she stepped out with?

"In dancing with Lord Brookmire, I do not consider myself unwise, Lord Cleverley."

Her short, sharp answer appeared to have caught his attention, for he immediately flushed and then dropped his gaze. His words did not cease, however.

"Perhaps it is that you have no awareness of the reputation of the gentleman who stands before you." Deborah sighed inwardly. She had thought that Lord Cleverley might apologize for his forwardness but, whether he realized it or not, he was once more insulting her by suggesting that she was either not intelligent enough, or considered enough to realize what she was doing.

"Lord Brookmire is a gentleman who holds the very worst of reputations. He is not a gentleman that any young lady ought to be considering." Lord Cleverley threw out one hand towards Lord Brookmire, his lips curving into a sneer. "And you, as a young lady of quality, ought not to even be conversing with Lord Brookmire, never mind dancing with him!"

Deborah put both hands on her hips, her anger rising quickly.

"And you are very forward with your opinions about what I should do, Lord Cleverley."

Her sharp retort had him again looking at her with wide eyes, his lips flattening as if he had only just realized precisely what he had said.

"I am only concerned for you, Miss Madeley."

Putting one hand to his heart, he went to say more, but Deborah cut him off with a swipe of her hand through the air between them.

"That may be so, but there are ways to discuss your concerns – none of which consist of dictating who I should speak with or dance with." Her eyes narrowed and her head tilted back a little, heat burning in her chest and, no doubt, sending fire into her expression. "I am sure that you mean well, but I am very well able to decide which persons I dance with, and which I do not."

"It may be that Lord Cleverley is correct, however." Lord Brookmire lifted his hands a little. "Mayhap it would be wiser for you to consider your own reputation when it comes to standing up with me. It was my mistake, Miss Madeley. I ought not to have asked."

More than a little frustrated by Lord Brookmire's change of heart, thanks solely to Lord Cleverley's interruptions, Deborah drew in a long breath, which she then let out slowly between clenched teeth in an attempt to rein in her still growing anger. Lord Cleverley was smiling delightedly, clearly pleased that his attempts to rescue Deborah had, in his mind, been very successful indeed. Lord Brookmire's head was lowering, his gaze turning to the ground, and Deborah's heart suddenly lurched.

"Is something amiss?"

Her mother's voice floated towards them and, turning her head, Deborah closed her eyes briefly, but said nothing. She had no need to, for Lord Cleverley had already interrupted with what sounded like an exclamation of victory.

"Lady Prescott! No, no, indeed, there is nothing of concern. I came upon your daughter, having heard her just accept Lord Brookmire's offer to dance, and was quickly able to inform her of the dangers of dancing with a gentleman who holds such a poor reputation. You will be glad to know that Lord Brookmire has rescinded his offer."

Lady Prescott's eyebrows lifted. She did not thank Lord Cleverley, nor did she berate Lord Brookmire for requesting such a thing from Deborah. Instead, she turned her gaze to Deborah, who again, remained silent. She did not know what to say, and feared that, if she were to speak honestly, nothing but fury would escape from her mouth and she would shame herself in front of both gentlemen and her mother.

"I see." Lady Prescott spoke slowly. "Lord Brookmire, you asked to dance with my daughter?"

He inclined his head.

"Forgive me, Lady Prescott. Mayhap I was little too hasty in my thinking. I had not thought about the damage it might cause Miss Madeley's reputation."

"As though you cared a jot about that!" Lord Cleverley's lip curled. "You only took back your offer once I was present. No doubt you do so now to save face, though why you should need to do such a thing given your standing in society, I cannot imagine."

Lord Brookmire's jaw jutted forward. His eyes narrowed a little and his face warmed but, much to Deborah's surprise, he did not respond to Lord Cleverley's caustic remarks. She glanced again at her mother, who was looking at Lord Brookmire with obvious interest, eyeing him carefully and seeing the same expression that Deborah considered.

Then, she smiled.

"I have no doubt, Lord Cleverley, that you meant well in speaking to my daughter so." Lord Cleverley immediately beamed, his smile spreading wide across his face, but Lady Prescott was not finished. "However." she continued, quickly, "my daughter does not require your advice nor your guidance. She has both myself and her father for such things and, while your input was well meant, I am sure, my daughter has already spoken to me about Lord Brookmire. It seems now that you and I do not share the same opinion." As Lord Cleverley's smile immediately changed to an expression of some startlement, Deborah's heart began to slow from the furious beat it had been pursuing. Her mother was not speaking sharply, but her words were firm enough for Lord Cleverley to realize that he had made a mistake. "Now, Lord Brookmire." Lady Prescott turned her attention to the other gentleman, who quickly lowered his head for a moment before returning his gaze to the lady. "I have heard from my daughter that you seek to reform yourself. I am not certain whether or not I fully believe this particular tale but, nonetheless, it is interesting for me to hear that a gentleman who has borne such a dreadful reputation now wishes to change. Lady Yardley accepts your word on it and, therefore, because of her standing and her trust in your promises, I have told Deborah that she may be in your company on occasion."

"You are more than generous, Lady Prescott." Lord Brookmire inclined his head again. "I can see where Miss Madeley gets her compassionate heart from. I am entirely undeserving – I am all too aware of that – and yet, Miss Madeley has been generous enough to offer me another opportunity, so that I might have a chance to prove myself and gain a stellar reputation rather than the dark one I currently bear."

Lady Prescott nodded and smiled.

"I am very pleased to hear it, Lord Brookmire." Smiling at Deborah, she caught her hand for a moment, pressing it lightly. "And you say that you wish to dance with Lord Brookmire, my dear? You wish to accept his offer?"

Deborah nodded firmly.

"Yes."

"Very well." Lady Prescott looked towards Lord Cleverley. "Again, I appreciate your concern for my daughter. However, she is more than able to make her own decisions in this regard. If she wishes to dance with Lord Brookmire, then I have no hesitation in allowing her to do so." Lord Cleverley looked away, and immediately began to stutter as he fought to find an answer. Scarlet filled his cheeks, his back was excessively straight, and his jaw tight, but nothing he tried to say made any sense. In the end, he simply dropped his head and shrugged. "As I have said," Lady Prescott murmured softly. "I understand your concern, but I believe that every person deserves an opportunity to prove themselves. Good evening, Lord Cleverley." She smiled at Deborah. "I shall be just over there, talking with Lady Venables, my dear."

Deborah heaved a sigh of relief, watching her mother walk away, and silently thinking her one of the most elegant, refined ladies she had ever known. After a breath, she looked towards Lord Cleverley. Her eyebrows lifted. Clearly, his anger had blossomed into fury, given the way that his hands were now clenched into fists and his furious gaze focused solely on Lord Brookmire.

"This is deeply unwise." His lip curled, and his jaw jutted forward as he turned his attention to Deborah. "I warn you, Miss Madeley. Should you step out with Lord Brookmire, then you and I shall no longer be of any interest to each other."

Deborah blinked.

"Do you think to threaten me, Lord Cleverley?"

There was no immediate flush of shame for, in fact, Lord Cleverley shrugged his shoulders as though it were more than justifiable to do such a thing.

"Call it what you will. I state, here and now, that I shall have no interest in *any* young lady whose decisions can be so foolishly made and whose reservations can be pulled aside by a charming smile."

Before Deborah could say anything in response, Lord Brookmire stepped closer.

"Forgive me, Miss Madeley." He then lifted both hands, his lips flat. "I did not mean to bring you such difficulty. I understand if it would be best for you not to –"

"It is not you who is causing difficulty, Lord Brookmire." Her head tilted, her eyes sliding back towards the other gentleman. "It is Lord Cleverley."

The gentleman rolled his eyes and Deborah had to use all of her strength simply to remain silent as she collected herself. How dismissively he had spoken to her! How little he seemed to think of her! In doing so, he had clearly shown that he thought himself above her, and he did not even seem to recognize it.

"Lord Cleverley." Her voice was shaking, and she dragged air into tight lungs. "Speaking to me as though I am a child in need of guidance is not something I appreciate from any gentleman. Threatening me is even *less* so. Do you truly think that I would wish to continue a connection with a gentleman who said such things, and who demanded all the more from me?" Lord Cleverley's haughty expression began to change, his chin lowering and his eyes darting away from her. He opened his mouth to speak, but Deborah shook her head, silently telling him that it was much too late to try to withdraw anything he had said. "Even when my own mother states that she has a different opinion from you, and has guided me herself, you attempt to insist that I follow *your* decrees rather than listen to the path my mother has set out for me. Is that how little you respect and regard her, Lord Cleverley? And is that how little you respect and regard me?"

His face slowly began to pale, clearly now realizing the

scale of the mistake he had made in speaking so, particularly as regarded Deborah's mother.

"I did not mean..." Closing his eyes, he pinched the bridge of his nose slightly. "I spoke hastily. I was a little upset, and I-"

"None of which matters." Deborah's decision was already made. "It seems as though our close acquaintance is at an end, Lord Cleverley. I *shall* be dancing with Lord Brookmire and therefore, as you yourself have said, we shall not be closely acquainted any longer." So saying, she took a small step closer Lord Brookmire before fixing Lord Cleverley with a sharp eye. "It seems as though we are not to have our phaeton ride together after all."

Lord Cleverley said nothing. He looked to her, then slid his gaze towards Lord Brookmire, only for the next dance to be announced. Deborah looked to Lord Brookmire expectantly, hoping that in the midst of all of this, he had not changed his mind out of concern for her.

Seeing her look, Lord Brookmire kept his voice low.

"If you still wish it then I would be more than happy to step out with you for this."

Deborah smiled, something warm curling in her belly.

"I thank you."

She accepted his arm and, with a small smile to Lord Cleverley, allowed herself to be led away from his company. The ending of her connection to Lord Cleverley was not something she mourned. Rather, she felt quite settled within herself, a peace stealing over her heart as though being on Lord Brookmire's arm was precisely where she'd always been meant to be.

CHAPTER THIRTEEN

*P*hillip smiled as Lord Marchmont handed him a brandy. They had only just arrived at the ball and Phillip had every intention of seeking out Miss Madeley just as soon as he could. Lord Marchmont, however, had been insistent on fetching them both a glass and thus, Phillip had waited patiently for his return.

"Thank you."

"But of course." Lord Marchmont lifted his glass in a half toast. "To your continued improvement." He grinned as Phillip arched an eyebrow. "I do not know the cause of this change, but I *have* seen you very altered these last few weeks. You spoke of some darkness, but I have seen some things in a bright light also." His head tilted. "And the cause of that is none other than Miss Madeley, it seems."

"She is very pleasing."

Phillip dared not say more than this, for to reveal his heart to Lord Marchmont when he himself had no clear understanding of precisely what it was that he felt would not be wise.

"And this is all you will say, then?" Lord Marchmont

chuckled. "If you are inclined towards the lady, there is no shame in that." He took a sip of his brandy, then chuckled again. "Even if you have been entirely disinclined towards such a thing before now."

"Yes, but I was a fool." Phillip spoke honestly, and Lord Marchmont's surprise etched itself into his features. "I did not realize the significance of having an interest in one soul alone, in feeling drawn to one particular person, over everyone else. It is both extraordinary and very confusing indeed."

Again, Lord Marchmont nodded, but this time, a smile came with it.

"She is a very lovely young lady with good connections and, from what I understand, something of a strength of character." Laughing, he shrugged, a question in his eyes. "Will you be able to be content with that?"

Phillip grinned.

"I think a strength of character a very fine thing." His smile softened a little. "Her heart is compassionate, her spirit nothing but sweetness. I feel a good deal for her, I confess it."

"It is Miss Madeley you speak of, is it not?"

Phillip's stomach turned over on itself as he turned sharply, seeing Lord Anderton standing behind them. How long had he been listening?

"Good evening, Lord Anderton." Lord Marchmont's tight voice offered an indication of his feelings. "Lord Brookmire and I were enjoying a private conversation. Do excuse us."

"It would be a shame if she should have her heart broken."

Lord Anderton shrugged both shoulders then looked away as Phillip's gaze shot straight to him. Surely, he could not mean to pull Miss Madeley into this dark endeavor!

"As I have said, Lord Anderton." Lord Marchmont's voice was firm. "This is a private conversation."

"And yet, Lord Brookmire is required to hear what I have to say." Coming to stand in between them, Lord Anderton only flicked his gaze towards Lord Marchmont for a moment, before fixing his beady eyes upon Phillip. "Lady Shawbost has recently expressed an interest in becoming a little better acquainted with you." Lord Anderton smiled as though he offered Phillip a great boon. "She is already in the gardens by the fountain. I said I would fetch you."

Instantly, Phillip shook his head.

"I have no interest in meeting Lady Shawbost. I will not go."

"You *shall*." Lord Anderton's voice was soft with danger. He waited a moment, then added, in an even quieter and more venomous tone, "Be advised that the Marquess of Harrogate is also present."

Phillip dropped his head, his heart pounding, his stomach lurching so furiously that he feared he might cast up his accounts.

"Brookmire?"

Lord Marchmont's gaze went from Phillip to Lord Anderton and back again, but Phillip did not have the heart to explain. What was it he would say? Did he tell his friend how foolish he had been? The depth of Lord Anderton's cruelty? It was too much to explain.

"She is waiting." Lord Anderton said it softly, putting one hand on Phillip's shoulder, and Phillip had to grit his teeth, restraining himself so that he would not knock it away. "I should go to her as soon as I could, if I were you.

After all, Miss Madeley is also in the gardens and my sole intention is for her to witness your... warmth towards Lady Shawbost. If she does not, then the very same situation will be set up again and again until it is complete – and should you warn her in the interim, then there will be a greater consequence for *her* to bear."

He moved away and Phillip let out a groan, which Lord Marchmont turned his attention towards, putting a hand on Phillip's arm as he squeezed his eyes closed. Dread began to fill his veins, turning him slowly to stone as Lord Marchmont searched his face.

"What is it that he demands of you? I do not understand."

There was no time to explain. He had no choice but to do as Lord Anderton asked, and this although everything in him rebelled furiously at the idea.

"You are my only hope, Marchmont." His voice hoarse as he spoke, he fixed his gaze on his friend. "Do one thing for me."

Lord Marchmont's eyes were steady on his.

"Anything."

"I have no doubt that Miss Madeley will have no interest in seeing me once she endures this pain." Slowly, his heart began to tear itself apart into as the impossibility of his situation pressed down upon him. "Please, speak to Miss Madeley. Tell her that Lord Anderton demanded it of me and that I was not in the least bit willing. She will know what it means... that is, so long as she is willing to even listen to you in the first place."

"You must explain this all to me." Lord Marchmont's tone lowered, his brow furrowing with lines. "Lord Anderton holds something over you, does he not?"

Phillip closed his eyes and breathed out slowly.

"This must be after I have introduced myself to Lady Shawbost. After that, I will explain all."

The pain in his chest only grew as he began to walk away, his steps dragging, his whole being demanding he stay still and allow the moment to pass but, clenching his teeth, Phillip forced one step after another, knowing that he had no other choice but to do as Lord Anderton had decreed.

Lord Marchmont did not come after Phillip as he walked away, clearly still deeply confused, but willing to do as Phillip had asked. How little he had appreciated his friend before now! His shame rose again, and he dropped his head, walking out into the gardens just as Lord Anderton had instructed. He did not look to the left, nor the right but made his way directly to the fountain, praying somehow, that Miss Madeley would not see him even if she was nearby. The gardens were well lit, and Phillip silently cursed the light, wishing he could wrap shadows around himself and hide everything which was about to occur from the lady he had taken into his heart.

"Lord Brookmire." Phillip's head lifted as Lady Shawbost's silken voice wrapped itself around him, tugging him closer. He did not move, his throat tight, his hands pulled into tight fists as his nails burned into his skin. *I do not want to do this.* "Silent?" Lady Shawbost giggled softly, then ran one hand up his arm. "One might enjoy a little entanglement out in the gardens and Lord Anderton told me that you would be more than willing." Her other hand went to his shoulder, then slipped around his neck, burning him. His eyes remained closed, his whole body beginning to shudder as he forced himself to remain in place while, at the same time, battling the desire to run from her with all the strength he possessed. "Why, you are as much of a scoundrel as has been said!" Lady Shawbost giggled again, pulling herself close to him, but Phillip did not so much as put one hand on her. "See how you shake with desire! We are so *very* much out in the open, however. I would have thought even a gentleman with a reputation such as yours would want to sneak away into the shadows!"

Phillip opened his mouth to say that he did not want to be here, and certainly did not want to have an entanglement with her in the middle of the gardens, only for Lady Shawbost to push herself up on tiptoe and press her mouth to his.

He pulled back instinctively, his head twisting sharply as a cry met his ears.

In the flickering light of the fire glow, Miss Madeley stood, watching. Her hand was at her mouth, her eyes wide – and instinctively, he went to her.

"Lord Brookmire!" Lady Shawbost pulled at his arm, but he shook her off. "That was not at all as I expected."

"Miss Madeley – Deborah!"

His hoarse voice barely made it through the darkness and before he could reach her, Miss Madeley turned into the arms of her friend and they both hurried away. His heart pounding, he made to follow her, only for Lady Shawbost to catch his arm again.

"Where are you going?"

Her voice had changed from its previous silken softness, and the whine grated across Phillip's broken spirits, sending yet more pain into his heart. He rounded on her.

"I am leaving, Lady Shawbost." Aware that he was responding harshly, Phillip did not hold himself back. "I did not come to be embraced by you for I have no interest in your company. Lord Anderton may have suggested otherwise, but the truth is, I have no desire to wrap my arms around you. Understand this, Lady Shawbost, I will not return, and I certainly will not give you what you seek."

Lady Shawbost blinked and made to say something, but Phillip was already turning back towards the ballroom. He did not know what he should do, or what he should say, but the desperate urgency to find Miss Madeley drove his every step. Heaving great breaths, he licked his lips, the shudder which had been in him before now strengthening all the more.

"Lord Brookmire." A quiet voice caught his attention and he turned, just as Lady Yardley caught his arm firmly. "Are you quite all right?"

"It is Deborah." A tightness rang through his voice as he continued his attempts to enter the ballroom, but Lady Yardley held him fast. "I have injured her. I must go and find her. I must-"

"*I* will speak with her." Lady Yardley held his gaze fixedly, her hand still restraining him. "You know that Lord Anderton will watch for you the moment that you step back into the ballroom. He will make certain that you do not go to Miss Madeley to explain. He wants you to feel this pain – and for her to feel it too. If you go to her now, I fear there will be consequences for you both." Phillip closed his eyes. "I should have considered this." Lady Yardley shook her head and turned it away, her expression tight. "I should have been more cautious and taken greater care with Lord Anderton, knowing that he might see the connection between you and Miss Madeley." Taking a breath, she looked at him again. "You can be assured that I will make certain that she knows your actions this evening were not done willingly."

A great fear now clung to Phillip's soul, sending a chill through him that brought gooseflesh to his skin.

"I do not think I can draw near her again." The realization of how much Lord Anderton might injure her, how much he could pull her into this darkness, suddenly over-whelmed him. "As much as I care for her, I do not want her to become a focus for Lord Anderton."

Much to Phillip's surprise, Lady Yardley smiled.

"And that speaks of true affection," she said softly, "but, knowing Miss Madeley as I do, I believe she will wish to make such a decision herself, once she knows all."

With a heavy sigh, Phillip nodded, closing his eyes as he did so.

"I cannot imagine how much I must have injured her."

His heart tore with a great pain, but Lady Yardley set a comforting hand on his for a moment.

"She will understand. The pain will fade." Her head tilted, and her eyes narrowed just a fraction. "You do truly care for her, do you not?"

Letting out a long breath, Phillip nodded.

"I have not wanted to admit it to anyone, wishing to resolve this situation with Lord Anderton before I looked to my own heart, but yes, it is as you say." His heart leaped despite the pain within it, and he managed a smile. "It is as if this difficulty has finally made me see how much I care for her. I am only sorry that my affection has become so obvious that Lord Anderton has used it against her."

"But he will not succeed." Lady Yardley spoke with a confidence that Phillip did not feel. "Have a little faith, Lord Brookmire. She will return to you."

CHAPTER FOURTEEN

*E*very part of her burned.

Her heart ached until she feared that she would be forced to cry out and reveal her pain. Everything within her was tying itself together, then exploding open again in fury, only to then repeat the same motion. She did not know where she was going, her eyes were fixed upon the floor as Lady Elizabeth led her forward.

Her mind screamed as the memory of what she had seen etched itself into her thoughts. Lord Brookmire had been playing the scoundrel – just as he was known to be. Had she been so easily deceived by him?

"Come, come." Lady Elizabeth led her to a quiet part of the ballroom, close to their mothers but far enough away that they would not be overheard. "You need something to drink. I shall fetch it. Wait a moment."

Deborah said nothing, sitting down in a chair near the wall of the ballroom and staring blankly straight ahead. She took in nothing, and tears pricked at the corners of her eyes. She seemed to have forgotten how to breathe and it was only when she recalled it, her lungs screaming for air, that she was finally able to draw breath. Deborah shuddered furiously, just as Lady Elizabeth handed her something cold and sweet to drink. Taking it, Deborah drank it all in only a few gulps, feeling the cool liquid washing through her and chasing away some of the fire which burned within her soul.

"It is very odd." Deborah looked at Lady Elizabeth, but her friend was looking away, her eyes on the ladies and the gentlemen dancing together. "Would a scoundrel be so obvious?"

"I beg your pardon?"

Everything in her shook with a mixture of fury, shock, and sorrow and, on seeing it, Lady Elizabeth flushed.

"Forgive me. It does not matter."

Squeezing her eyes closed tightly, Deborah gestured towards her friend.

"Please. What is it that you meant?"

With a sigh, Lady Elizabeth spread out one hand.

"It is only an idle thought. I know that he is a scoundrel, and scoundrels are less than considered when it comes to their reputation, but I would have thought that he might have hidden himself a little more. The gardens were well-lit with those torches, and I am surprised that he thought to take Lady Shawbost into his arms in such an obvious fashion. It was as though he *wanted* to be seen." Something caught tight in Deborah's chest. She fixed such a sharp gaze upon Lady Elizabeth and looked at her for so long without saying a single word, that Lady Elizabeth eventually flapped with one hand and looked away. "No doubt I am being foolish. I should not expect Lord Brookmire to behave in any fashion other than that of a rogue."

Swallowing hard, Deborah rubbed her hand over her eyes. Was there any truth in what Lady Elizabeth had suggested? Lord Brookmire *had* been very obvious - more than obvious, in fact. It was, as Lady Elizabeth had said, as if he had wanted her to see him.

No. Surely it cannot be!

Her head dropped forward, and she let out a long, low groan. Lady Elizabeth was beside her at the very next moment, an arm going around her shoulders.

"You must feel a great deal of pain, Deborah. I ought not to have said a word."

"No. It is not that." Again, Deborah lifted her gaze to Lady Elizabeth, seeing the concern sparkling in her friend's eyes. Tears of relief now began to edge towards her eyes, and she managed a wobbly laugh. "It is not that I am distressed. It is quite the opposite."

Handing her a handkerchief, Lady Elizabeth said nothing, taking a seat next to Deborah and waiting for her to explain.

"Lady Elizabeth, Miss Madeley."

Before Deborah could begin to express what she now believed, none other than Lord Marchmont appeared. He was grim-faced, his mouth set into a tight line, his brows low and his sharp inclination of his head speaking of haste,

"Excuse the interruption." His hands clasped behind his back. "I confess, I am greatly confused but I have a message for you from Lord Brookmire. He begged me to find you and to inform you that he was forced into this action – an action to do with Lady Shawbost, I think?" His brows lowered all the more, drawing a heavy line between them. "Lord Anderton came to speak with us and stated that Lady Shawbost was waiting. Lord Brookmire was entirely disinclined to go to her, but Lord Anderton, in some way or other, forced his hand. Lord Anderton demanded that he do such a thing solely to injure you, I think, Miss Madeley. Does Lord Anderton have something against you?"

Deborah's eyes closed. It was exactly as she had begun to believe. Lord Brookmire had not behaved in this way deliberately but had been forced to do so by Lord Anderton.

"He does not have something against me, but he holds a great deal of power over Lord Brookmire."

Lady Elizabeth caught her breath, her hand going to her mouth, just as Lady Yardley came over to join them. Putting her hand on Deborah's shoulder, she bent down just a little, searching her face.

"I see Lord Marchmont has already spoken to you." Lady Yardley glanced over her shoulder to the gentleman, then back to Deborah. "I have come to make certain that you know that what you witnessed of Lord Brookmire was—"

"Demanded by Lord Anderton." Deborah managed a wry smile as Lady Yardley nodded. "After Lady Elizabeth made some remark about how it was as though Lord Brookmire had wanted to be seen, I began to wonder if Lord Anderton had insisted that he do this particular thing."

Lord Marchmont cleared his throat.

"He was deeply troubled over how much he will have injured you. I was made to promise that I would find you and tell you all."

Comforted by this, Deborah rose to her feet.

"I do not doubt that Lord Anderton will be currently delighting in his victory, however, whilst Lord Brookmire is utterly wretched." Her chin lifted. "I confess that I have had quite enough." A sudden flurry of strength rippled through her and, with her hands spread wide, she looked to Lady Yardley. "There must be something we can do to stop Lord Anderton. He will continue to hold this over Lord

Brookmire's head for the remainder of his days if he so wishes, and I cannot bear to see it. In addition, I also remain concerned for Lady Gwendoline, who will also be threatened by Lord Anderton, whether she is aware of it or not. I am certain that there are many other gentlemen, and even ladies, whom Lord Anderton currently holds in his power. Surely there is something that we can do which will force him to stop such behavior! If we free Lord Brookmire, that does not solve the true source of the difficulty. Lord Anderton will continue to behave as he has always done, and those he chooses from amongst the *ton* will find themselves trapped and struggling."

"There are others." Lord Marchmont glanced at Lady Yardley, then to Deborah. "I know of some who have concerns over Lord Anderton, and remain far from him. I have always thought him a dangerous fellow."

"And are some here this evening?" As Lord Marchmont nodded 'yes', Lady Yardley took a deep breath and let it out in a sudden huff. "Very well. There is one thing we can do. I have been thinking about, but I considered it a little too risky."

"But we must try, I think." Deborah saw the flash in Lady Yardley's eyes and, after a moment, caught her small smile. "I admire your strength. Might you be willing to find Lord Brookmire? I warned him to stay away from you for the moment but, if we are to remove Lord Anderton's power, then he must see you together. It will show Lord Anderton that his plan to break you both has not succeeded, which will, of course, bring him a great deal of frustration – and frustration can be used to our advantage."

Deborah nodded, her eyes a little wider as she clasped her hands tightly together.

"You think that we can bring Lord Anderton to the end of his power?"

It took a few moments but, eventually, Lady Yardley nodded.

"Yes. It will require strength, courage, and certainly a good deal of boldness but, if Lord Brookmire is willing, then I hope that we will find ourselves holding the victory."

Having very little idea of what it was that Lady Yardley intended, Deborah smiled, grateful that her mother had always encouraged her to be bold and courageous, rather than shrinking back.

"I will find him at once." She looked to Lady Elizabeth "Might you accompany me?"

Her friend joined her at once, and the two fell into step together. Deborah's heart began to beat furiously as they walked in silence, surrounded by the hubbub of the ball. Her eyes searched every corner and peered into every shadow, her free hand pulling into a tight fist and then releasing slowly as anticipation and worry wound themselves tightly together and shot sparks through her veins. Her whole body was trembling lightly and, as they began the slow return to Lady Yardley, Deborah began to fear that he had already left the ball... only to set eyes upon the very gentleman she had been seeking.

"Lord Brookmire."

Breathing his name, she stopped suddenly, taking him in as relief washed through her. To her eyes, he appeared utterly wretched, his head bowed forward, his hair in disarray as he scraped his fingers through it once more. He was shaking his head and muttering to himself and, as she approached, his head lifted. Rounded eyes looked back at her, and there was a heaviness about his white face, his shoulders drooping low, then, as she came closer, he closed his eyes.

"Deborah." The soft voice which reached her came from a broken man "Please do not turn from me now. I swear to you, I had no willingness nor desire for Lady Shawbost. I may have appeared a scoundrel but I-"

"Brookmire." Heedless to those around her and forgetting even about Lady Elizabeth, Deborah put one hand out and caught his. Immediately Lord Brookmire's gaze flew to hers, and he blinked furiously as she smiled at him. "Pray, do not fear for even a moment. I realize now that Lord Anderton was doing what he could to break both your heart and mine – no doubt, simply to be spiteful." She took a breath. "However, if we do not do something of significance then he will continue along this path, injuring as many people as he wishes. Therefore, we must find a way to bring an end to his power."

For some moments, Lord Brookmire did not speak. His fingers curled tightly around hers and he gazed back into her face as though not really seeing her. It was only when she smiled and squeezed his hand that he dropped his head, letting out a heavy breath with it.

"Can this be true?" His voice wavered slightly. "Is it truly you, Miss Madeley? Are you truly present, standing here, telling me that I have nothing to fear?"

"You have not lost me." Still smiling, she moved a little closer, wishing it was only she and Lord Brookmire standing together. "But we must be courageous, Lord Brookmire. We must find a way to end Lord Anderton's tight grip upon you, and upon the others he reigns over. If you have courage, Lady Yardley has an idea. Thereafter, perhaps we might speak together about... some more personal things." Her face warmed as he closed his eyes briefly again, only for a smile to cross his face. "Will you come with me, Brookmire?"

His eyes opened, and Lord Brookmire then gazed deeply into her eyes. After a moment he reached out with one hand and brushed his fingers lightly down her cheek.

"I would follow you to the very end of the earth if it was asked of me," he murmured softly, sending her heart into a burst of overwhelming joy. "Take me to Lady Yardley. I shall do whatever is required if it means that I can be free to live without fear. I hope that my future will be a little brighter because of it."

"I shall stand with you, regardless of what takes place," she promised him, softly. "You mean too much to my heart for me to ever step back from you."

Lord Brookmire lifted her hand and pressed a kiss to the back of it, the softness of his lips sending such a wave of heat through her, she lost all strength for just a moment and his grip upon her hand was the only thing to steady her.

"It has taken almost losing you to make me realize how much I feel." His gentle whisper was like the roar of the wind, her hand clinging to his as she saw the truth in his eyes. "We shall speak later, Deborah, so I might confess all."

She swallowed, her whole body burning with anticipation.

"I shall confess to you also, Brookmire. But for the moment, let us go."

≈

"Lord Brookmire." Lady Yardley's shoulders lowered in evident relief. "I am glad to see that you have not left the ball."

Phillip offered a small smile, inclining his head.

"I had thought to do that very thing, Lady Yardley, but I was prevented by my melancholy." Looking towards Miss Madeley, he considered for a moment how his heart had broken when he had been forced to embrace Lady Shaw-bost. It had been in that moment that his heart had revealed itself fully, showing him that there was love for Miss Madeley present within it and thus, he had been torn asunder at her cry of horror. How he wished he'd had the opportunity to both understand this situation and to tell her of it before this moment! "I am also grateful to Miss Madeley for allowing me to explain myself."

Her hand still rested on his arm, although they were not walking together. Her gentle smile healed the lingering wounds within him, knowing now that he had nothing to fear. She trusted him., she believed his words, and he was nothing but grateful.

"I have no doubt that Lord Anderton will be most displeased to see you together in such a fashion." A small smile crossed Lady Yardley's face, her eyes twinkling. "But we shall use that to our advantage."

Phillip nodded. He had very little idea of what Lady Yardley had planned, for it was all coming upon him so quickly, but both she and Miss Madeley were correct. They could not simply allow Lord Anderton to continue in such a fashion. The fact that he had sought to injure Miss Madeley had been a step too far and, therefore, if something was to be done tonight against Lord Anderton, so be it.

"Lord Harrogate is here this evening." Lady Yardley lifted her chin and set a firm gaze upon Phillip. "Can you be bold, Lord Brookmire? Can you be honest?"

Phillip struggled to answer, a familiar fear returning to his mind as he looked at Miss Madeley.

"I do wish to be," he murmured, turning his attention to

Lady Yardley and seeing from both her smile and the softness about her eyes that she understood his fear exactly. "I do not want to be separated from Miss Madeley because of it, however."

"I will tell my mother all if I must." Miss Madeley's determination was an encouragement to him. "She has always taught me to know my own mind. I do not think that she would allow any truth to be a bar between us. Rather, if you were to tell her all for the sake of our connection, she would accept it as a mark of genuine affection."

Phillip heaved a breath.

"Very well." With new confidence loosening the tightness in his limbs, he looked to Lady Yardley. "What is it that must be done?"

Lady Yardley smiled briefly, then turned her attention to Lord Marchmont.

"Lord Marchmont, might you do me a particular favor?"

Phillip watched as his friend nodded, realizing now how fortunate he was to have the friendship of this gentleman, for Lord Marchmont had nodded immediately, his willingness clear.

"Of course. Anything you wish."

Lady Yardley smiled.

"I thank you. Firstly, might you find any gentlemen you know who have been injured by Lord Anderton? If they are present this evening, ask them to join us in our conversation with Lord Harrogate, stating that it will be an opportunity to steal away Lord Anderton's power. I will bring Lord Yardley, and Lord Sherbourne also, if he can be found. Thereafter..." Taking a breath, she paused for a moment, "This may sound a little strange but pray, find Lord Anderton. Tell him that we are discussing his good name with the Marquess of Harrogate."

"You will need to give me a few minutes to find these gentlemen." Lord Marchmont's jaw tightened. "I know there are some gentlemen here who are afraid of Lord Anderton. They will not tell me why, but mayhap they can be persuaded if I am to say that his cruelties are to be revealed."

Despite his trust in her, Phillip's heart leaped to hear what Lady Yardley's intention was, aware of the consequences of such an endeavor, especially should anything fail. All the same, he did not say a word against the plan but instead, pressed Miss Madeley's hand.

"I hope that this will be successful and that Lord Anderton will be reined in." Keeping his voice low so only Miss Madeley could hear him, he smiled, but with a sense of sadness in his heart. "But if it is not and if, thereafter, we are to be separated, I hope that you know how much my heart clings to you."

"Oh, Lord Brookmire." Her eyes shone and the love in his heart exploded into a rolling ball of flame that ran from his chest all the way down to his toes. "We will not be separated." Her quiet words were filled with a confidence that Phillip did not share. "For what can separate two hearts which are so completely entwined?"

There was no time for him to consider what she meant by those words for, at that moment, Lady Yardley bade them all to go in search of Lord Harrogate while she went to find her husband. Hesitating, he paused, took Miss Madeley's hand, and pressed a kiss to the back of it.

Then, without a word, he tucked her hand under his arm and went in search of the Marquess of Harrogate.

CHAPTER FIFTEEN

"*L*ord Harrogate."

Much to Phillip's relief, Lord Harrogate did not appear to be in his cups, in any way whatsoever, as Lady Yardley greeted him. He held a glass of something which looked like brandy, but it was barely touched.

"Lady Yardley!" The Marquess smiled broadly, bowing towards her. "It is a pleasure to see you again, I do not think that we have had the opportunity to converse so far this Season. I am sure that my wife would be very happy to be in your company also. You cannot know how much we both admire your endeavor with 'The London Ledger'!"

"You are very kind." She gestured to her husband. "You are acquainted with my husband as well, I think?"

"Yes, of course."

Phillip took in the scene as Lord Harrogate's eyes went first to Lord Yardley, then to Miss Madeley, and finally, to Phillip himself. Bowing, Phillip greeted him quietly, aware that the man's smile had dimmed a little.

"Regrettably, I do come with grave news, rather than to make pleasant conversation." Lady Yardley spoke directly, choosing to go straight into the conversation about Lord Anderton, rather than enquiring after his family or the like. "It does, unfortunately, involve your daughter." Lord Harrogate's eyebrows immediately flew towards his hairline while, at the next moment, his eyes swiveled towards Phillip. Lady Yardley, catching this, set a hand to the gentlemen's arm for a second. "Do not judge Lord Brookmire harshly, I beg of you, for it is not he who is to blame."

Her soft voice and Lord Yardley's firm nod appeared to take some of the instant fury away from Lord Harrogate's face, for his eyebrows drew low again and he looked to Lady Yardley instead of glaring at Phillip. Trying to appear as calm as he could, Phillip winced at the cold sweat which had broken out across his forehead. A dull ache began to throb in his temples, firing an ache into every one of his muscles.

"This is to do with Lord Anderton."

When Lord Yardley spoke those words the Marquess of Harrogate's eyes flared in response.

"Lord Anderton?" the Marquess replied, frowning. "I do not know the gentleman particularly well. What has he done to my daughter? And why would he do anything to injure her – if that is what you imply?"

"It is not what he has done, but what he threatens." Lady Yardley shook her head sorrowfully, then put out a hand towards Phillip. "As unpleasant as this is to hear, Lord Anderton has been threatening your daughter's reputation, albeit without her knowledge." In an instant, Lord Harrogate sucked in a breath, his shoulders tensing a little. Phillip cleared his throat, going to speak, but Lady Yardley's small shake of her head silenced him. "I shall explain." Lady Yardley again gestured towards Phillip, who felt Miss Madeley's hand curve more tightly around his arm.

Whether it came from a sense of solidarity, or from anxiety, he was not certain, but he appreciated her nearness all the same. "Lord Brookmire, as you may know, has recently determined to reform himself. He is a gentleman who has something of a poor reputation at present and he will admit to that."

"Yes."

Nodding fervently, Phillip had again opened his mouth but only managed that one word before snapping it closed as Lady Yardley continued.

"Lord Anderton, however, took an opportunity to create a situation in which he might blackmail Lord Brookmire. In knowing Lord Brookmire's reputation, he stated that one of the ladies whom Lord Brookmire embraced *before* he decided to change his ways was, in fact, your daughter, Lady Gwendoline." Heat began to billow across the Marquess' face. His jaw tightened, his jaw clenched, and he shot a narrowed gaze toward Phillip. But again, Lady Yardley put a hand on his arm. "Understand that Lord Anderton likes to blackmail and deceive." Lady Yardley stayed away from stating outright that Phillip had, in fact, kissed Lord Harrogate's daughter and, given the situation, doing so seemed very wise indeed. What she had said was enough for Lord Harrogate to understand, without putting even a spot of shame upon his daughter's reputation.

"I assure you that I have never willingly sought out your daughter." At this juncture, Phillip could not help but speak, choosing truth where he could find it. "Lord Anderton, however, stated that it was *your* daughter whom I embraced one evening and, though I tried to argue with him, he stated, quite clearly, that if I did not do as he required, he would inform the *ton* of it. He was more than willing to ruin not only my reputation but also the reputation of your daughter."

Lord Harrogate sucked in a breath, his face paling.

"Is this true?" He looked at Lady Yardley, then Lord Yardley before setting a steely gaze on Phillip again. "Why would he do such a thing?"

"Because he is not the gentleman he seems." It was Miss Madeley who spoke now, sounding as firm as Lady Yardley had done. "Lord Anderton appears to be a jovial, mirthful gentleman, but in truth, he has injured many. He keeps a tight hold over those he wishes to control, and he does so rather successfully."

Something ticked in Lord Harrogate's cheek and, much to Phillip's relief, he did not immediately demand retribution, as he had feared might be the case. Instead, he took in a long, steadying breath, briefly closed his eyes, and then spoke again.

"You attest to this, Lord Yardley?"

Lord Yardley nodded.

"I do indeed. I was forced to come to the aid of Lord Brookmire for, in becoming aware of his difficulties with Lord Anderton, I sought to help him, alongside Lord Sherbourne, who will tell you the same. We did not wish for any of Lord Anderton's endeavors to be successful."

Lord Harrogate folded his arms.

"I see."

Phillip spoke up again, a growing desperation within him to have Lord Harrogate believe him.

"I do not shy away from the fact that I was a scoundrel. I can understand why you might be unwilling to believe that I have changed my character, but that is the truth of it. I will hold to the truth that I cared little for others and did only as I pleased, but now, a good many things have happened which have altered me. I am not the gentleman I wish to be, and I have no desire to cling to the reputation I own. I have been endeavoring to change and, in doing so, have found a happiness I never anticipated might be offered to me. I have found kindness, compassion, and even affection." A glance at Miss Madeley sent a warm smile spreading across her cheeks, and it took a moment for Phillip to regain himself. With another breath, he looked back at Lord Harrogate, holding himself tall. "Lord Anderton has been attempting to injure not only myself, but others also, simply for the pleasure of doing so. He even set me against my friend, and had it not been for Lord Yardley and Lord Sherbourne, he might have succeeded. This evening he sought to injure Miss Madeley and again, thanks to the endeavor of my friends, and the trust she has in me, he has failed."

"But we cannot permit him to continue in such a way." Lady Yardley held out both hands. "This is why we pray that you believe us, and will set your face against Lord Anderton."

Lord Harrogate cleared his throat, shrugged, and then threw out his hands.

"I have no cause to doubt you, Lady Yardley." His brow furrowed as he looked at Phillip. "You, however, I do not trust."

"And I do not hold that against you," Phillip answered, honestly. "Why should anyone such as yourself trust me? Do not accept my words but, in listening to Lady Yardley, Lord Yardley, and Miss Madeley, I pray that their words say something about my change in character being genuine."

Lord Harrogate's frown lifted a little.

"It is Lord Anderton who is the rogue here," Miss Madeley murmured, quietly. "If he can use this situation to his own advantage, then he will act upon it. If he can lie, then the words will be spoken without a moment's thought. If he can cheat, then he shall and if he can blackmail, he will not even hesitate."

"Whatever is this?" Lord Anderton suddenly blustered into the group surrounding Lord Harrogate, glaring hard at Phillip before he turned his attention to the Marquess. "I am afraid, Lord Harrogate, I have something of the greatest concern to tell you. Lord Brookmire is, no doubt, attempting to explain himself away but–"

"Lord Anderton." Miss Madeley interrupted his monologue, her hands going to her hips. "It has already been explained and there is no need for you to say anything more. Lord Harrogate is already aware of your cruelties."

Lord Anderton dismissed her with a snort and a wave of his hand.

"I am afraid that Miss Madeley is rather overcome by Lord Brookmire's presence. No doubt she thinks him more than eager for her company but, alas, she will soon find out the truth about his character." Heaving a sigh, he sent her a cold look. "No doubt, in a short while, Lord Brookmire will dismiss her and then she will wonder why she ever believed a single word that he said to her."

Miss Madeley let out an exclamation of fury, but Lord Harrogate was the one to speak.

"You are a little dismissive of Miss Madeley, I think." Tilting his head, he gestured to Lord and Lady Yardley. "Will you dismiss Lord and Lady Yardley's remarks about you also?"

"Given that I do not know what has been said, I find that I cannot say whether or not I..." He was a little uncertain of himself, trying to smile as his eyes danced from Lord Yardley to Lady Yardley and back again. "However, I should remind you, Lord Harrogate, that Lord Brookmire is a gentleman well known to be able to twist people into doing whatever he wishes."

"Even someone such as Lady Yardley?" Lord Harrogate lifted his eyebrows. "I find it very surprising indeed that you would even suggest such a thing! Lady Yardley is well respected and known to take great care in all she hears and considers, especially given that she writes 'The London Ledger'. I think her very well-reasoned in everything."

"Ah, but–"

"I have something I can tell you about Lord Anderton also."

Turning his head, Phillip smiled in relief as Lord Marchmont approached, interrupting Lord Anderton. It was not only he, however, but six other gentlemen and one lady who walked with him.

"You are not coming to speak against me, are you?" Lord Anderton threw up his hands. "It was you who told me of this conversation and–"

Lord Marchmont ignored Lord Anderton entirely, looking straight at Lord Harrogate.

"I am afraid that it is as Lord Brookmire has said. No doubt Lady Yardley has told you that Lord Anderton is a cruel sort, and I am here to concur with her in that. He will do whatever he wishes to gain whatever he can for himself. I was witness to one such scheme last year, during the Season. An unfortunate gentleman who attempted to take part in a race was grievously injured – and Lord Anderton demanded his payment while the man was still on his sickbed."

Several gentlemen murmured their agreement at this, and Lord Harrogate's eyes flew wide.

"Lord Anderton has been forcing me to do his bidding, but it was he who cheated me out of a great amount of coin.

As yet, I have not been able to repay it, for he continued to add more debt to it – and he also threatens to expose my ruination to all should I say a word."

It was a grey-haired gentleman who had spoken clearly and, as Phillip watched, another gentleman stepped forward also.

"He did the same to me. I discovered later that he had placed something in my whisky which made me greatly confused. However, since I could not prove such a thing and, given that I now owe him a great deal, he has forced me to do as he requires."

"And he has attempted to ruin my sister." A gentleman Phillip recognized as Lord Stonefield jabbed one finger in Lord Anderton's direction, his face almost purple with obvious fury. "He states that she was in a particular situation - a situation my darling sister denies, begging me to believe her – but Lord Anderton ignores this. Instead, he tells me that he will inform her betrothed of what he has heard about her unless I do as he asks."

A sense of relief began to fill Phillip's heart, and he closed his eyes briefly before turning his attention to Lord Anderton. No longer was he a man filled with confidence. Instead, his eyes were wide and, after rubbing them hard with one hand, he blinked slowly, as if hardly able to accept that this was the situation in which he found himself. It was clear that he had always expected that these gentlemen - Phillip included - would do as they were bid, and never say a single word to anyone. The fact that they had now banded together to speak the truth was something entirely unexpected and as such, Lord Anderton had very little idea what he ought to do. At this expression, Phillip found himself smiling.

Surely, it must be over.

Lord Harrogate's gruff cough caught everyone's attention. Miss Madeley's hand found Phillip's and he held it tightly in his own, certain that the same tension which ran through him also flew through her. What was Lord Harrogate's judgment to be?

"There can be no doubt." Lord Harrogate's voice gathered those not involved in the conversation to him, with many other guests from the ball now intrigued by what was to be said. Phillip held his breath, his chest tight, his heart pounding... and Lord Harrogate caught his eye. "I believe every word that Lady Yardley has said. These gentlemen make it clear to me that Lord Anderton has behaved despicably, and not in the way expected of a gentleman."

Phillip closed his eyes tightly, hearing Miss Madeley's ragged gasps and wishing desperately that he could pull her into his arms. The judgment had fallen – and it had fallen in Phillip's favor.

"You ought to be hounded out of London, Lord Anderton."

The rasping anger in Lord Harrogate's voice had Lord Anderton beginning to back away, his hands raised in a weak attempt to defend himself, a plea upon his lips, a whiteness beginning to push color away from his face, but no one was listening to him.

"How dare you attempt to smear the name of my daughter?" Lord Harrogate continued, now thunderous in his anger. "How dare you attempt to use her in such an underhanded manner? And even worse, you have attempted to steal the honor of each of these gentlemen, simply for your own gain!" His jaw worked furiously. "Something must be done about you."

"If I may?" As Lord Anderton continued to splutter beside him, Phillip gestured to Lady Yardley. "I believe that

Lady Yardley does an excellent job as regards 'The London Ledger'. It is a trusted publication in London. Might it be that any gentleman or lady who has been so treated by Lord Anderton might speak to Lady Yardley, to express what has taken place?"

"So that she might, in turn, report of these circumstances in the Ledger," Lord Harrogate finished, clearly catching upon the idea with great speed as Lord Anderton let out a low groan of dismay, one hand now over his eyes as though shutting out the sight of those who condemned him would save him. "Yes, I think that is an excellent suggestion."

The Marquess smiled briefly but then turned his fierce gaze back to Lord Anderton, who wilted like a plant which had seen no rain in some time. Phillip slowly stepped back, Miss Madeley's hand still in his as they moved away. There was nothing left for him to say, nothing more he wished to discuss, nothing more he had to mention. The only person he wished to speak with now was Miss Madeley.

"Good gracious! Whatever has taken place here? And were you a part of it?"

The voice of Lady Prescott broke between them, and Phillip caught the fact that her eyes immediately went to where her daughter's hand was wrapped around his. Quickly disentangling himself, Phillip took a step away from Miss Madeley and bowed quickly.

"Forgive me, Lady Prescott. I am sure that your daughter will tell you all, but I shall excuse myself for the remainder of the evening." Seeing Miss Madeley's longing look, he smiled softly. "Mayhap I might call upon you tomorrow, Miss Madeley?"

She nodded, her eyes never leaving his.

"I am already counting the moments until your arrival."

Her soft words made his heart leap, and he bowed low again, feeling himself unworthy of her, but overwhelmingly grateful at the same time.

"I will not be tardy, not even by a single second."

He smiled at her once more, before finally stepping away, resisting the urge to pull her into his arms. As he turned, he caught sight of Lord Marchmont, his arms folded as he waited for Phillip to join him.

"Mayhap *now* you will explain to me precisely what it is that has taken place?" Lord Marchmont grinned ruefully. "It is not to say that I am not pleased that Lord Anderton has been removed from his position of power, only that I have very little idea of what it was that he held over you."

Phillip slapped his friend on the shoulder.

"Yes, of course, I shall explain all. I do hope, however, that you know how grateful I am to you for your assistance this evening."

Lord Marchmont smiled.

"But of course. I do hope that you and Miss Madeley will be very happy together. I assume you will propose to her very soon?"

Grinning, Phillip nodded, his heart filled with a sudden joy as if fireworks were exploding all around him.

"I shall," he swore. "I fully intend to declare myself to her tomorrow and I can only pray that she will accept me."

EPILOGUE

"*L*ord Brookmire, my Lady."

Deborah turned from where she had been standing at the window, her hands immediately clasping at her heart. Her mother had warned her that she would only be absent for a few short minutes, clearly aware that her daughter and Lord Brookmire had some words to share. It was only now that Deborah felt a sudden rush of nerves flooding her and, as Lord Brookmire stepped into the room, she suddenly did not know where to look.

"Miss Madeley - Deborah."

Lord Brookmire put an end to her nervousness by striding across the room and taking her hand, his confidence chasing away her nervousness. His touch set her body aflame, her heart yearning to be closer to this gentleman than she had ever been before. The look in his eyes compelled her to step closer and, as she did so, Lord Brookmire's sigh of relief had her melting into his arms.

"I do not deserve this." His voice was soft in her ear, his words holding so much truth, she closed her eyes to focus upon them with all of her strength. "I am not a gentleman worthy of the gift you offer me, Miss Madeley. You have shown me loyalty when I deserved none. You have shown me strength when you had no need to stand by my side and you have offered me a companionship which you could have – you ought to have - given to any other present here in London. There are many gentlemen more worthy of all you offer than I."

She pulled back, looking up into his face, daring herself to be bold. Her fingers skimmed across his cheek before brushing through his hair, and she smiled at his startled breath.

"And yet, no other has taken my heart."

Her truth was laid out bare for him to see and, as his eyes searched hers, Deborah simply smiled, praying he would believe that she spoke honestly. When he closed his eyes and gave a short shake of his head, her smile dimmed for fear that his heart quailed, only for his arms to wrap a little more tightly about her waist as he pulled her gently against him.

"It is because of you that I want to become the very best of gentlemen." One hand ran lightly up and down her back and she rested her head upon his shoulder, hearing the steady beat of his heart. "You challenged me to believe that I can be more than I ever thought. I want my name to be respected so that *you* are honored." When his fingers ran over the nape of her neck, Deborah shivered lightly and looked up at him, her own heart seeming to tremble at the promise in his eyes. "I will honor you in everything."

Lord Brookmire's words had her heart leaping with a furious joy and fervent hope. She licked her lips, waiting and, as Lord Brookmire dropped his head, everything within her cried out with anticipation. He did not kiss her, however, waiting for her to be the one to touch her mouth to his, honoring her even in that. With an eagerness she had never known she possessed, Deborah stood on tiptoe and kissed the gentleman she loved.

Fire enveloped her and she caught her breath, sensations flooding every part of her being. Lord Brookmire broke their kiss quickly, her name whispered against her lips and, when he cradled her face with one hand, she sighed contentedly.

"I do not know if your father will agree, but I want to offer you my hand." His lips curved into a wry smile as she held his gaze steadily. "It may take some convincing, but I am willing to prove myself." A brief touch of his lips seared her again. "The only thing I wish to do for the rest of my days is learn how to love you better every day. My hope is to be the very best of gentlemen so that I might be the very best husband to you. I love you, Deborah. I love *only* you and I shall be devoted to you for the rest of my days."

Her heart exploded with happiness and, with a quiet laugh, she draped her arms around his neck again.

"My dear Brookmire," she answered, pulling herself as close to him as she could. "I am sure that we can convince my father. Yes, it may take a little time, but I will not be separated from you. The gentleman I once pushed away is the only one I now desire to be near." Again she lifted herself up on her toes so that she might kiss him again, her heart overflowing with all that she felt. "I love you, Brookmire. I shall love you always."

I HOPE Lord Brookmire becomes everything he promised and more for Deborah!

.   .   .

DID you miss the first book in the **Only for Love** series? The Heart of a Gentleman Read ahead for a sneak peek!

READ THESE BOOKS? Like Governesses and Companions? Here is the boxset for that series! Ladies on their Own Boxset

MY DEAR READER

Thank you for reading and supporting my books! I hope this story brought you some escape from the real world into the always captivating Regency world. A good story, especially one with a happy ending, just brightens your day and makes you feel good! If you enjoyed the book, would you leave a review on Amazon? Reviews are always appreciated.

Below is a complete list of all my books! Why not click and see if one of them can keep you entertained for a few hours?

The Duke's Daughters Series
The Duke's Daughters: A Sweet Regency Romance Boxset
A Rogue for a Lady
My Restless Earl
Rescued by an Earl
In the Arms of an Earl
The Reluctant Marquess (Prequel)

A Smithfield Market Regency Romance
The Smithfield Market Romances: A Sweet Regency
Romance Boxset
The Rogue's Flower
Saved by the Scoundrel
Mending the Duke
The Baron's Malady

The Returned Lords of Grosvenor Square
The Returned Lords of Grosvenor Square: A Regency
Romance Boxset
The Waiting Bride
The Long Return
The Duke's Saving Grace
A New Home for the Duke

The Spinsters Guild
The Spinsters Guild: A Sweet Regency Romance Boxset
A New Beginning
The Disgraced Bride
A Gentleman's Revenge
A Foolish Wager
A Lord Undone

Convenient Arrangements
Convenient Arrangements: A Regency Romance
Collection
A Broken Betrothal
In Search of Love
Wed in Disgrace
Betrayal and Lies
A Past to Forget
Engaged to a Friend

Landon House
Landon House: A Regency Romance Boxset
Mistaken for a Rake
A Selfish Heart
A Love Unbroken
A Christmas Match
A Most Suitable Bride

An Expectation of Love

Second Chance Regency Romance
Second Chance Regency Romance Boxset
Loving the Scarred Soldier
Second Chance for Love
A Family of her Own
A Spinster No More

Soldiers and Sweethearts
To Trust a Viscount
Whispers of the Heart
Dare to Love a Marquess
Healing the Earl
A Lady's Brave Heart

Ladies on their Own: Governesses and Companions
Ladies on their Own Boxset
More Than a Companion
The Hidden Governess
The Companion and the Earl
More than a Governess
Protected by the Companion

Lost Fortunes, Found Love
A Viscount's Stolen Fortune
For Richer, For Poorer
Her Heart's Choice
A Dreadful Secret
Their Forgotten Love
His Convenient Match

Only for Love

The Heart of a Gentleman
A Lord or a Liar
The Earl's Unspoken Love
The Viscount's Unlikely Ally

Christmas Stories
Love and Christmas Wishes: Three Regency Romance
Novellas
A Family for Christmas
Mistletoe Magic: A Regency Romance
Heart, Homes & Holidays: A Sweet Romance Anthology

Happy Reading!
All my love,
Rose

A SNEAK PEEK OF THE
HEART OF A GENTLEMAN

CHAPTER ONE

"Thank you again for sponsoring me through this Season." Lady Cassandra Chilton pressed her hands together tightly, a delighted smile spreading across her features as excitement quickened her heart. Having spent a few years in London, with the rest of her family, it was now finally her turn to come out into society. "I would not have been able to come to London had you not been so generous."

Norah, Lady Yardley smiled softly and slipped her arm through Cassandra's.

"I am just as glad as you to have you here, cousin." A small sigh slipped from her, and her expression was gentle. "It does not seem so long ago that I was here myself, to make my Come Out."

Cassandra's happiness faded just a little

"Your first marriage was not of great length, I recall." Pressing her lips together immediately, she winced, dropping her head, hugely embarrassed by her own forthrightness "Forgive me. I ought not to be speaking of such things."

Thankfully, Lady Yardley chuckled.

"You need not be so concerned, my dear. You are right to say that my first marriage was not of long duration, but I *have* found a great happiness since then - more than that, in fact. I have found a love which has brought me such wondrous contentment that I do not think I should ever have been able to live without it." At this, Cassandra found herself sighing softly, her eyes roving around the London streets as though they might land on the very gentleman who would thereafter bring her the same love, within her own heart, that her cousin spoke of. "But you must be cautious," her cousin continued. "There are many gentlemen in London – even more during the Season – and not *all* of them will seek the same sort of love match as you. Therefore, you must always be cautious, my dear."

A little surprised at this, Cassandra looked at her cousin as they walked along the London streets.

"I must be cautious?"

Her cousin nodded sagely.

"Yes, most careful, my dear. Society is not always as it appears. It can be a fickle friend." Lady Yardley glanced at Cassandra then quickly smiled - a smile which Cassandra did not immediately believe. "Pray, do not allow me to concern you, not when you have only just arrived in London!" She shook her head and let out an exasperated sigh, evidently directed towards herself. "No doubt you will have a wonderful Season. With so much to see and to enjoy, I am certain that these months will be delightful."

Cassandra allowed herself a small smile, her shoulders relaxing in gentle relief. She had always assumed that London society would be warm and welcoming and, whilst there was always the danger of scandal, that danger came only from young ladies or gentlemen choosing to behave improperly. Given that she was quite determined *not* to behave so, there could be no danger of scandal for her!

"I assure you, Norah, that I shall be impeccable in my behavior and in my speech. You need not concern yourself over that."

Lady Yardley touched her hand for a moment.

"I am sure that you shall. I have never once considered otherwise." She offered a quick smile. "But you will also learn a great deal about society and the gentlemen within it – and that will stand you in good stead."

Still not entirely certain, and pondering what her cousin meant, Cassandra found her thoughts turned in an entirely new direction when she saw someone she recognized. Miss Bridget Wynch was accompanied by another young lady who Cassandra knew, and with a slight squeal of excitement, she made to rush towards them – somehow managing to drag Lady Yardley with her. When Cassandra turned to apologize, her cousin laughingly disentangled herself and then urged Cassandra to continue to her friends. Cassandra did so without hesitation and, despite the fact it was in the middle of London, the three young ladies embraced each other openly, their voices high with excitement. Over the last few years, they had come to know each other as they had accompanied various elder siblings to London, alongside their parents. Now it was to be their turn and the joy of that made Cassandra's heart sing.

"You are here then, Cassandra." Lady Almeria grasped her hand tightly. "And you were so concerned that your father would not permit you to come."

"It was not that he was unwilling to permit me to attend, rather that he was concerned that he would be on the continent at the time," Cassandra explained. "In that regard, he was correct, for both my father *and* my mother

eave of England, and have gone to my father's
n the continent. I am here, however, and stay
... with my cousin." Turning, she gestured to Lady Yardley who was standing only a short distance away, a warm smile on her face. She did not move forward, as though she was unwilling to interrupt the conversation and, with a smile of gratitude, Cassandra turned back to her friends. "We are to make our first appearances in Society tomorrow." Stating this, she let out a slow breath. "How do you each feel?"

With a slight squeal, Miss Wynch closed her eyes and shuddered.

"Yes, we are, and I confess that I am quite terrified." Taking a breath, she pressed one hand to her heart. "I am very afraid that I will make a fool of myself in some way."

"As am I," Lady Almeria agreed. "I am afraid that I shall trip over my gown and fall face first in front of the most important people of the *ton*! Then what shall be said of me?"

"They will say that you may not be the most elegant young lady to dance with?" Cassandra suggested, as her friends giggled. "However, I am quite sure that you will have a great deal of poise – as you always do – and will be able to control your nerves quite easily. You will not so much as stumble."

"I thank you for your faith in me."

Lady Almeria let out a slow breath.

"Our other friends will be present also," Miss Wynch added. "How good it will be to see them again – both at our presentation and at the ball in the evening!"

Cassandra smiled at the thought of the ball, her stomach twisting gently with a touch of nervousness.

"I admit to being excited about our first ball also. I do

wonder which gentlemen we shall dance with." Lady Almeria swiveled her head around, looking at the many passersby before leaning forward a little more and dropping her voice low. "I am hopeful that one or two may become of significant interest to us."

Cassandra's smile fell.

"My cousin has warned me to be cautious when it comes to the gentlemen of London." Still a little disconcerted by what Lady Yardley had said to her, Cassandra gave her friends a small shrug. "I do not understand precisely what she meant, but there is something about the gentlemen of London of which we must be careful. My cousin has not explained to me precisely what that is as yet, but states that there is much I must learn. I confess to you, since we have all been in London before, for previous Seasons – albeit not for ourselves – I did not think that there would be a great deal for me to understand."

"I do not know what things Lady Yardley speaks of," Miss Wynch agreed, a small frown between her eyebrows now. "My elder sister did not have any difficulty with *her* husband. When they met, they were so delighted with each other they were wed within six weeks."

"I confess I know very little about Catherine's engagement and marriage," Lady Almeria replied, speaking of her elder sister who was some ten years her senior. "But I *do* know that Amanda had a little trouble, although I believe that came from the realization that she had to choose which gentleman was to be her suitor. She had *three* gentlemen eager to court her – all deserving gentlemen too – and therefore, she had some trouble in deciding who was best suited."

Cassandra frowned, her nose wrinkling.

"I could not say anything about my brother's marriage, but my sister did wait until her second Season before she accepted a gentleman's offer of courtship. She spoke very little to me of any difficulties, however - and therefore, I do not understand what my cousin means." A small sigh escaped her. "I do wish that my sister and I had been a little closer. She might have spoken to me of whatever difficulties she faced, whether they were large or small, but in truth, she said very little to me. Had she done so, then I might be already aware of whatever it is that Lady Yardley wishes to convey."

Miss Wynch put one hand on her arm.

"I am sure that we shall find out soon enough." She shrugged. "I do not think that you need to worry about it either, given that we have more than enough to think about! Maybe after our come out, Lady Yardley will tell you all."

Cassandra took a deep breath and let herself smile as the tension flooded out of her.

"Yes, you are right." Throwing a quick glance back towards her cousin, who was still standing nearby, she spread both hands. "Regardless of what is said, I am still determined to marry for love."

"As am I." Lady Almeria's lips tipped into a soft smile. "In fact, I think that all of us – our absent friends included – are determined to marry for love. Did we not all say so last Season, as we watched our sisters and brothers make their matches? I find myself just as resolved today as I was then. I do not think our desires a foolish endeavor."

Cassandra shook her head.

"Nor do I, although my brother would have a different opinion, given that he trumpeted how excellent a match he made with his new bride."

With a wry laugh, she tilted her head, and looked from one friend to the other.

"And my sister would have laughed at us for such a

suggestion, I confess," Lady Almeria agreed. "She states practicality to be the very best of situations, but I confess I dream of more."

"As do I." A slightly wistful expression came over Miss Wynch as she clasped both hands to her heart, her eyes closing for a moment. "I wish to know that a gentleman's heart is filled only with myself, rather than looking at me as though I am some acquisition suitable for his household."

Such a description made Cassandra shudder as she nodded fervently. To be chosen by a gentleman simply due to her father's title, or for her dowry, would be most displeasing. To Cassandra's mind, it would not bring any great happiness.

"Then I have a proposal." Cassandra held out her hands, one to each of her friends. "What say you we promise each other – here and now, that we shall *only* marry for love and shall support each other in our promises to do so? We can speak to our other friends and seek their agreement also."

Catching her breath, Lady Almeria nodded fervently, her smile spreading across her face.

"It sounds like a wonderful idea."

"I quite agree." Miss Wynch smiled back at her, reaching to grasp Cassandra's hand. "We shall speak to the others soon, I presume?"

"Yes, of course. We shall have a merry little band together and, in time, we are certain to have success." Cassandra sighed contentedly, the last flurries of tension going from her. "We will all find ourselves suitable matches with gentlemen to whom we can lose our hearts, knowing that their hearts love us in return."

As her friends smiled, Cassandra's heart began to soar. This Season was going to be an excellent one, she was sure.

Yes, she had her cousin's warnings, but she also had her friends' support in her quest to find a gentleman who would love her; a gentleman she would carry in her heart for all of her days. Surely such a fellow would not be so difficult to find?

CHAPTER TWO

"*I* should like to hear something... significant... about you this Season."

Jonathan rolled his eyes, knowing precisely what his mother expected. This was now his fourth Season in London and, as yet, he had not found himself a bride – much to his mother's chagrin, of course. On his part, it was quite deliberate and, although he had stated as much to his mother on various occasions, it did not seem to alter her attempts to encourage him toward matrimony.

"You are aware that you did not have to come to London with me, Mother?" Jonathan shrugged his shoulders. "If you had remained at home, then you would not have suffered as much concern, surely?"

"It is a legitimate concern, which I would suffer equally, no matter where I am!" his mother shot back fiercely. "You have not given me any expectation of a forthcoming marriage and I continually wonder and worry over the lack of an heir! You are the Marquess of Sherbourne! You have responsibilities!"

Jonathan scowled.

"Responsibilities I take seriously, Mother. However, I will not be forced into–"

"I have already heard whispers of your various entanglements during last Season. I can hardly imagine that this Season will be any better."

At this, Jonathan took a moment to gather himself, trying to control the fierce surge of anger now burning in his soul. When he spoke, it was with a quietness he could barely keep hold of.

"I assure you, such whispers have been greatly exaggerated. I am not a scoundrel."

He could tell immediately that this did not please his mother, for she shook her head and let out a harsh laugh.

"I do not believe that," she stated, her tone still fierce. "Especially when my *dear* friend, Lady Edmonds, tells me that you were attempting to entice her daughter into your arms!" Her eyes closed tight. "The fact that she is still willing to even be my friend is very generous indeed."

A slight pang of guilt edged into Jonathan's heart, but he ignored it with an easy shrug of his shoulders.

"Do you truly think that Lady Hannah was so unwilling? That I had to coerce her somehow?" Seeing how his mother pressed one hand to her mouth, he rolled his eyes for the second time. "It is the truth I tell you, Mother. Whether you wish to believe me or not, any rumors you have heard have been greatly exaggerated. For example, Lady Hannah was the one who came to seek *me* out, rather than it being me pursuing her."

His mother rose from her chair, her chin lifting and her face a little flushed.

"I will not believe that Lady Hannah, who is so delicate a creature, would even have *dreamt* of doing such a thing as that!"

"You very may very well not believe it, and that would not surprise me, given that everyone else holds much the same opinion." Spreading both hands, Jonathan let out a small sigh. "I may not be eager to wed, Mother, but I certainly am not a scoundrel or a rogue, as you appear to believe me to be."

His mother looked away, her hands planted on her hips, and Jonathan scowled, frustrated by his mother's lack of belief in his character. During last Season, he had been utterly astonished when Lady Hannah had come to speak with him directly, only to attempt to draw him into some sort of assignation. And she only in her first year out in Society as well! Jonathan had always kept far from those young ladies who were newly out – even, as in this case, from those who had been so very obvious in their eagerness. No doubt being a little upset by his lack of willingness, Lady Hannah had gone on to tell her mother a deliberate untruth about him, suggesting that *he* had been the one to try to negotiate something warm between them. And now, it seemed, his own mother believed that same thing. It was not the first time that such rumors had been spread about gentlemen – himself included and, on some occasions, Jonathan admitted, the rumors had come about because of his actions. But other whispers, such as this, were grossly unfair. Yet who would believe the word of a supposedly roguish gentleman over that of a young lady? There was, Jonathan considered, very little point in arguing.

"I will not go near Lady Hannah this Season, if that is what is concerning you." With a slight lift of his shoulders, Jonathan tried to smile at his mother, but only received an angry glare in return. "I assure you that I have no interest in Lady Hannah! She is not someone I would consider even stepping out with, were I given the opportunity." Protesting his innocence was futile, he knew, but yet the words kept coming. "I do not even think her overly handsome."

"Are you stating that she is ugly?"

Jonathan closed his eyes, stifling a groan. It seemed that he could say nothing which would bring his mother any satisfaction. The only thing to please her would be if he declared himself betrothed to a suitable young lady. At present, however, he had very little intention of doing anything of the sort. He was quite content with his life, such as it was. The time to continue the family line would come soon enough, but he could give it a few more years until he had to consider it.

"No, mother, Lady Hannah is not ugly." Seeing how her frown lifted just a little, he took his opportunity to escape. "Now, if you would excuse me, I have an afternoon tea to attend." His mother's eyebrows lifted with evident hope, but Jonathan immediately set her straight. "With Lord and Lady Yardley," he added, aware of how quickly her features slumped again. "I have no doubt that you will be a little frustrated by the fact that my ongoing friendship with Lord and Lady Yardley appears to be the most significant connection in my life, but he is a dear friend and his wife has become so also. Surely you can find no complaint there!" His mother sniffed and looked away, and Jonathan, believing now that there was very little he could say to even bring a smile to his mother's face, turned his steps towards the door. "Good afternoon, Mother."

So saying, he strode from the room, fully aware of the heavy weight of expectation that his mother continually placed upon his shoulders. He could not give her what she wanted, and her ongoing criticism was difficult to hear. She did not have proof of his connection to Lady Hannah but, all the same, thought poorly of him. She would criticize his close acquaintance with Lord and Lady Yardley also! His friendships were quickly thrown aside, as were his explanations and his pleadings of innocence - there was nothing he could say or do that would bring her even a hint of satisfaction, and Jonathan had no doubt that, during this Season, he would be a disappointment to her all over again.

"Good afternoon, Yardley."

His friend beamed at him, turning his head for a moment as he poured two measures of brandy into two separate glasses.

"Sherbourne! Good afternoon, do come in. It appears to be an excellent afternoon, does it not?"

Jonathan did so, his eyes on his friend, gesturing to the brandy on the table.

"It will more than excellent once you hand me the glass which I hope is mine."

Lord Yardley chuckled and obliged him.

"And yet, it seems as though you are troubled all the same," he remarked, as Jonathan took a sip of what he knew to be an excellent French brandy. "Come then, what troubles you this time?" Lifting an eyebrow, he grinned as Jonathan groaned aloud. "I am certain it will have something to do with your dear mother."

Letting out an exasperated breath, Jonathan gesticulated in the air as Lord Yardley took a seat opposite him.

"She wishes me to be just as you are." Jonathan took a small sip of his brandy. "Whereas I am less and less inclined to wed myself to *any* young lady who has her approval... simply because she will have my mother's approval!"

Lord Yardley chuckled and then took a sip from his

glass.

"That is difficult indeed! You are quite right to state that *you* will be the one to decide when you wed... so long as it is not simply because you are avoiding your responsibilities."

"I am keenly aware of my responsibilities, which is precisely *why* I avoid matrimony. I already have a great deal of demands on my time – I can only imagine that to add a wife to that burden would only increase it!"

"You are quite mistaken."

Jonathan chuckled darkly.

"You only say so because your wife is an exceptional lady. I think you one of the *few* gentlemen who finds themselves so blessed."

Lord Yardley shrugged.

"Then I must wonder if you believe the state of matrimony to be a death knell to a gentleman's heart. I can assure you it is quite the opposite."

"You say that only because you have found contentment," Jonathan shot back quickly. "There are many gentlemen who do not find themselves so comfortable."

Lord Yardley shrugged.

"There may be more than you know." He picked up his brandy glass again. "And if that is what you seek from your forthcoming marriage to whichever young lady you choose, then why do you not simply search for a suitable match, rather than doing very little other than entertain yourself throughout the Season? You could find a lady who would bring you a great deal of contentment, I am sure."

Resisting the urge to roll his eyes, Jonathan spread both hands, one still clutching his brandy, the other one empty.

"Because I do not feel the same urgency about the matter as my mother," he stated firmly. "When the time is right, I will find an excellent young lady who will fill my heart with such great affection that I will be unable to do anything but look into her eyes and find myself lost. *Then* I will know that she is the one I ought to wed. However, until that moment comes, I will continue on, just as I am at present." For a moment he thought that his friend would laugh at him, but much to his surprise, Lord Yardley simply nodded in agreement. There was not even a hint of a smile on his lips, but rather a gentle understanding in his eyes which spoke of acceptance of all that Jonathan had said. "Let us talk of something other than my present situation." Throwing back the rest of his brandy, and with a great and contented sigh, Jonathan set the glass back down on the table to his right. "Your other guests have not arrived as yet, I see. Are you hoping for a jovial afternoon?"

"A cheerful afternoon, certainly, although we will not be overwhelmed by too many guests today." Lord Yardley grinned. "It is a little unfortunate that I shall soon have to return to my estate." His smile faded a little. "I do not like the idea of being away from my wife, but there are many improvements taking place at the estate which must be overseen." His lips pulled to one side for a moment. "Besides which, my wife has her cousin to chaperone this Season."

"Her cousin?" Repeating this, Jonathan frowned as his friend nodded. "You did not mention this to me before."

"Did I not?" Lord Yardley replied mildly, waving one hand as though it did not matter. "Yes, my wife is to be chaperoning her cousin for the duration of the Season. The girl's parents are both on the continent, you understand, and given that she would not have much of a coming out otherwise, my wife thought it best to offer."

Jonathan tried to ignore the frustration within him at the fact that his friend would not be present for the Season, choosing instead to nod.

"How very kind of her. And what is the name of this cousin?"

"Lady Cassandra Chilton." Lord Yardley's gaze flew towards the door. "No doubt you will meet her this afternoon. I do not know what is taking them so long but, then again, I have never been a young lady about to make her first appearance in Society."

Jonathan blinked. Clearly this was more than just an afternoon tea. This Lady Cassandra would be present this afternoon so that she might become acquainted with a few of those within society. Why Lord Yardley had not told him about this before, Jonathan did not know – although it was very like his friend to forget about such details.

"Lady Cassandra is being presented this afternoon?"

His friend nodded.

"Yes, as we speak. I did offer to go with them, of course, but was informed she was already nervous enough, and would be quite contented with just my dear wife standing beside her."

Jonathan nodded and was about to make some remark about how difficult a moment it must be for a young lady to be presented to the Queen, only for the door to open and Lady Yardley herself to step inside.

"Ah, Lord Sherbourne. How delighted I am to see you."

With a genuine smile on her face, she waved at him to remain seated rather than attempt to get up to greet her.

"Good afternoon, Lady Yardley. I do hope the presentation went well?"

"Exceptionally well. Cassandra has just gone up to change out of her presentation gown – those gowns which the Queen requires are so outdated and uncomfortable! She will join us shortly."

The lady threw a broad smile in the direction of her

husband, who then rose immediately from his chair to go towards her. Taking her hands, he pressed a kiss to the back of one and then to the back of the other. It was a display of affection usually reserved only for private moments, but Jonathan was well used to such things between Lord and Lady Yardley. In many ways, he found it rather endearing.

"I am sure that Cassandra did very well with you beside her."

Lady Yardley smiled at her husband.

"She has a great deal of strength," she replied, quietly. "I find her quite remarkable. Indeed, I was proud to be there beside her."

"I have only just been hearing about your cousin, Lady Yardley. I do hope to be introduced to her very soon." Shifting in his chair, Jonathan waved his empty glass at Lord Yardley, who laughed but went in search of the brandy regardless. "You are sponsoring her through the Season, I understand."

His gaze now fixed itself on Lady Yardley, aware of that soft smile on her face.

"Yes, I am." Settling herself in her chair, she let out a small sigh as she did so. "I have no doubt that she will be a delight to society. She is young and beautiful and very well-considered, albeit a little naïve."

A slight frown caught Jonathan's forehead.

"Naïve?"

Lady Yardley nodded.

"Yes, just as every young lady new to society has been, and will be for years to come. She is quite certain that she will find herself hopelessly in love with the very best of a gentleman and that he will seek to marry her by the end of the Season."

"Such things do happen, my dear."

Lady Yardley laughed softly at Lord Yardley's remark, reaching across from her chair to grasp her husband's hand.

"I am not saying that they do not, only that my dear cousin thinks that all will be marvelously well for her in society and that the *ton* is a welcoming creature rather than one to be most cautious of. I, however, am much more on my guard. Not every gentleman who seeks her out will be looking to marry her. Not every gentleman who seeks her out will believe in the concept of love."

"Love?" Jonathan snorted, rolling his eyes to himself as both Lord and Lady Yardley turned their attention towards him. Flushing, he shrugged. "I suppose I would count myself as someone who does not believe such a thing to have any importance. I may not even believe in the concept!"

Lady Yardley's eyes opened wide.

"You mean to say that what Lord Yardley and I share is something you do not believe in?"

Blinking rapidly, Jonathan tried to explain, his chest suddenly tight.

"No, it is not that I do not believe it a meaningful connection which can be found between two people such as yourselves. It is that I personally have no interest in it. I have no intention of marrying someone simply because I find myself in love with them. In truth, I do not know if I am even capable of such a feeling."

"I can assure you that you are, whether or not you believe yourself to be."

Lord Yardley muttered his remark rather quietly and Jonathan took in a slow breath, praying that his friend would not start instructing him on the matter of love."

Lady Yardley smiled and gazed at Jonathan for some moments before taking a breath and continuing.

"All the same, I do want my cousin to be cautious, particularly during this evening's ball. I want her to understand that not every gentleman will be as she expects."

"I am sure such gentlemen will make that obvious all by themselves."

This brought a frown to Lady Yardley's features, but a chuckle came from Lord Yardley instead. Jonathan grinned, just as the door opened and a young lady stepped into the room, beckoned by Lady Yardley. A gentle smile softened her delicate features as she glanced around the room, her eyes finally lingering on Jonathan.

"I feel as though I have walked into something most mysterious since everyone stopped talking the moment I entered." One eyebrow arching, she smiled at him. "I do hope that someone will tell me what it is all about!"

Jonathan rose, as was polite, but his lips seemed no longer able to deliver speech. Even his breath seemed to have fixed itself inside his chest as he stared, his mouth ajar, at the beautiful young woman who had just walked in. Her skin was like alabaster, her lips a gentle pink, pulled into a soft smile as blue eyes sparkled back at him. He had nothing to say and everything to say at the very same time. Could this delightful young woman be Lady Yardley's cousin? And if she was, then why was no one introducing him?

"Allow me to introduce you." As though he had read his thoughts, Lord Yardley threw out one hand towards the young woman. "Might I present Lady Cassandra, daughter to the Earl of Holford. And this, Lady Cassandra, is my dear friend, the Marquess of Sherbourne. He is an excellent sort. You need have no fears with him."

Bowing quickly towards the young woman, Jonathan fought to find his breath.

"I certainly would not be so self-aggrandizing as to say

that I was 'an excellent sort', Lady Cassandra." he was somehow unable to draw his gaze away from her, and his heart leaped in his chest when she smiled all the more. "But I shall be the most excellent companion to you, should you require it, just as I am with Lord and Lady Yardley."

There was a breath of silence, and Jonathan cleared his throat, aware that he had just said more to her than he had ever said to any other young lady upon first making their acquaintance. Even Lord Yardley appeared to be a little surprised, for there was a blink, a smile and, after another long pause, the conversation continued. Lady Yardley gestured for her cousin to come and sit beside her, and the young lady obliged. Jonathan finally managed to drag his eyes away to another part of the room, only just becoming aware of how frantically his heart was beating. Everything he had just said to his friend regarding what would occur should he ever meet a young lady who stole his attention in an instant came back to him. Had he meant those words?

Giving himself a slight shake, Jonathan settled back into his chair, lost in thought as conversation flowed around the room. This was nothing more than an instant attraction, the swift kick of desire which would be gone within a few hours. There was nothing of any seriousness in such a swift response, he told himself. He had nothing to concern himself with and thus, he tried to insert himself back into the conversation just as quickly as he could.

Oh, no, Jonathan likes her! Perhaps he will have to change his mind about becoming leg-shackled! Check out the rest of story in the Kindle Store The Heart of a Gentleman

JOIN MY MAILING LIST

Sign up for my newsletter to stay up to date on new releases, contests, giveaways, freebies, and deals!

Free book with signup!

Monthly Facebook Giveaways! Books and Amazon gift cards!
Join me on Facebook: https://www.
facebook.com/rosepearsonauthor

Website: www.RosePearsonAuthor.com

Follow me on Goodreads: Author Page

Printed in Great Britain
by Amazon

26222249R00126